Storm Constantine's Wraeththu Mythos

Voices of the Silicon Beyond

OTHER BOOKS BY E. S. WYNN

A Selection from His Works

From Thunderune Publishing

Gold Hills, Rust Valley: 20 Tales
from Post-Apocalyptic California
Astride Twin Seas
Black Magic: Shotgun Spacebabe
Rise of the Forgotten God
Cinder Block Houses
Red Gender
The Way It Must Be

Wraeththu Mythos from Immanion Press

Whispers of the World That Was
Echoes of Light and Static

Storm Constantine's Wraeththu Mythos

Voices of the Silicon Beyond

Book Three of 'The Gold Country' Series

E. S. Wynn

IMMANION
PRESS

Stafford, England

Storm Constantine's Wraeththu Mythos:
Voices of the Silicon Beyond (Book Three of 'The Gold Country' Series)
By E. S. Wynn
copyright © 2018 Storm Constantine and E. S. Wynn

Cover Art: Ruby
Wraeththu Mythos Logo: Ruby
Interior Layout: Storm Constantine

Set in Palatino Linotype

IP0148

ISBN 978-1-907737-97-8

An Immanion Press Edition
http://www.immanion-press.com
info@immanion-press.com

THE HISTORY OF WRAETHTHU
A NEWCOMER'S GUIDE

(Updated introduction from book two of
'The Gold Country Series')

Storm Constantine

The novels set within the Wraeththu Mythos are published with the intention that they be accessible to everyone, whether or not they have read any of the preceding books and stories. This introduction is provided to give readers new to the Mythos an overview of the Wraeththu world and how it's evolved, and I hope it will also be of interest to long-standing fans.

The Wraeththu Mythos stories first appeared in print in 1987, with the publication of *'The Enchantments of Flesh and Spirit'*, which was the initial volume in the trilogy *'The Wraeththu Chronicles'*, but I'd written stories about these beings since I was a teenager. The book – when published – was described as 'ground breaking' because of some of genre taboos it challenged. They opened up new territory for genre fiction. *'Enchantments'* was followed by the final two installments of the trilogy: *'The Bewitchments of Love and Hate'* (1988) and *'The Fulfilments of Fate and Desire'* (1989). The books were published by Macdonald in the UK and TOR in America.

Wraeththu are a race that has sprung from the ruins of human civilization after humanity has all but destroyed its own environment. Wraeththu are androgynous – having both male and female physical aspects. Their sexuality is a source of power, an ability to transcend mundane reality as well as being an extremely spiritual practice.

While androgynes had been seen in science fiction and – more rarely – fantasy before, they had never been explored in such a way as I sought to explore them. Hara – as Wraeththu are known – have a deep connection with what we term magic and are more powerful in many respects than humans. Warriors and sorcerers, farmers and diplomats; familiar roles perhaps, but robed in very different forms.

Initially, hara were created through a mutation; Wraeththu blood could transform a human into a har. Once they became established, they were able to breed, (in fact had to learn how to do so), and a new generation of 'pure born' rather than incepted hara was created.

Other aspects that set the books apart from typical fantasy was that their environment was influenced heavily by the alternative music scene of the 1980s and 90s, as well as Paganism, which was becoming more acceptable in mainstream society as a belief system. Hara were flamboyant peacocks and fierce urban shamans, evolving from feral tribes of the disaffected young of humankind. When the books were first published, these were not characters typically found in fantasy fiction.

In the initial trilogy, I explored the questions that interested me: were Wraeththu the world's revenge on its savage, selfish children, or were they perhaps the outcome of a scientific experiment, designed to save the human race, that went wrong?

From the very start, something within Wraeththu – perhaps my own love of that world and its inhabitants – captured the hearts of many fans, who remained loyal to it, even when for over fifteen years I didn't write any new Wraeththu stories. Fans kept it alive through fan fiction – creating their own stories set within the Mythos.

Throughout the 90s and 2000s, Wraeththu's fandom continued to grow and thrive. I returned to writing within the Mythos with the publication of *'The Wraiths of Will and Pleasure'* in 2003, the first of *'The Wraeththu Histories'*, (followed by *'The Shades of Time and Memory'* (2004) and *'The Ghosts of Blood and Innocence'* (2005)). I've since written three more Wraeththu novels – the Alba Sulh sequence, which includes *'The Hienama'*, (2005) *'Student of Kyme'* (2008) and *'The Moonshawl'* (2014), a stand-alone triptych of novellas entitled *'Blood, the Phoenix and a Rose'* (2016) and two collections of short stories *'A Raven Bound with Lilies'* (2017) and *'Songs to Earth and Sky: Stories of the Seasons'* (2017), the latter written with several other Mythos writers.

The first Wraeththu shared world novel was *'Breeding Discontent'*, by Wendy Darling and Bridgette Parker (2003). This was followed by *'Terzah's Sons'* by Victoria Copus (2005) and *'Song of the Sulh'* by Maria J Leel (2012), and E.S. Wynn's 'The Gold Country Series', comprising *'Whispers of the World That Was'*, (2015) *'Echoes of Light and Static'* (2017) and this concluding volume in the series.

Immanion Press has also published several short story anthologies edited by Wendy Darling and me. Details of all Mythos titles can be found at the end of this book.

'Voices of the Silicon Beyond' is the latest Wraeththu Mythos novel and continues E. S. Wynn's investigation of the hara of the Gold Country. Writers always work with 'what ifs?' In E. S. Wynn's case, this was: what if incepted hara could

not accept their new state of being and tried to deny it? What if such hara existed within a landscape that had for some time been isolated and estranged from humanity even before humans lost their hold on the world? What if...?

Many of those questions were answered in *'Whispers of the World That Was'*, and the author took the idea further in *'Echoes of Light and Static'*, revealing what happens when hara of the most advanced tribe, the Gelaming, come across the hara of the Gold Country, where something very strange indeed continues to haunt the landscape and the lives of the hara who live there.

In this final volume, Vaetta, a female synthetic human known as a Valkyrie – far more than a mere robot – travels through a newly-opened, cross-realm conduit to the world of Wraeththu. In her reality, hara don't exist and those who created her see Wraeththu only as diseased mutants, the result of a plague that destroyed humankind on their Earth. To the people who hold power in Vaetta's overpopulated, dying world, this new Earth is merely a resource to plunder and colonize. Vaetta and her fellow Valkyries are, in effect, the vanguard of an invasion. This is a threat Wraeththu could never have imagined, but what Vaetta finds on the other side of the conduit is far beyond her expectations too.

E. S. Wynn – whose work has also been published in Wraeththu Mythos anthologies – brings a fresh new voice to the world of hara. This is a voyage of discovery – for the characters and readers alike.

CHAPTER 1

Vaetta. Hey, how soon can you get down here?

The silicon lattice meshed into my mind wakes up before I do. My eyes open, but it takes a moment before I see. A simulation of the smell of coffee blossoms in my mind, freshly brewed, and the sensation of having just finished it tricks the rest of my brain into sudden awareness. I sit up, pick the sleep from my eyes with precise, practiced motions and think words into the comm channel that John has already opened.

Ten minutes. Fifteen if there's traffic.

There's always traffic. John transmits back, his thoughts forming words in my mind. *I'll tell Chief that you'll be here in twenty.*

I close the channel with a thought, a single mote in a cluster of thoughts, and each mote triggers a dozen changes in my body, in the world around me. I stand, and at the same instant that the light coming through the single window of my one-room cube apartment lightens and turns a soft and subtle shade of blue, the sides and surface of my bed collapse themselves, fold into a shape the size of a piece of paper that blends seamlessly with the wall. Tiny electromagnetic field emitters laced into layers of my skin spin up an illusion of clothing so real it fools even me sometimes. The warmth, the fit, the sensation of fabric on my skin—it's perfect. By the time I turn to face the window, catch my reflection there, my eyes are already blue, the striking, icy shade I've come to favor, and my midnight hair has already laced itself into a business-like and conservative bun.

Breakfast is a jet injection, painless, bloodless and efficient. It feels like a luxury to stop for a moment and sip a glass of water afterward. One of the few indulgences I've come to allow myself as I've gotten older. Even then, in those precious seconds, I flick through a series of pre-set looks for the projected clothing I wear, make the most of it. Flicking through colors, brilliant blues and clashing reds, I ultimately settle back to something more neutral, something simple for the walk to Grey Division. The emitters in my skin spin up the illusion of a basic ankle-length skirt thick enough to keep out the cold, top it with a button-up blouse and a cardigan, all in shades of slate. A quick query on the weather outside shows the usual. Light rain, light ash. Twelve degrees Celsius, thirty-two percent relative humidity, forty-six percent relative mist toxicity.

Down six percent from yesterday, I note. I try not to think too much about the corresponding drop in the economy that has probably come with it. *Could be wind*, I tell myself. *More likely a mining hive gone quiet.*

Last time, it was a mining hive gone quiet.

Briefly, I recall something Chief once said, about how the world has gone to shit. I wouldn't know. It's not for me to say. This world is the only world I've ever known. The people, the endless throngs of surging people, the weight and mass of humanity pressing in on the skin of the Earth, the sky choked with the exhausted toxins of human industry and progress. Fifty years ago, cities had names, boundaries, spaces to separate them. Fifty years ago, there were nations, borders, places where the sprawl and the toxins came to an end, places untouched by human innovation. Now, humanity lives in an interconnected webwork of districts and zones governed by a hungry elite class. Any place that is not too polluted to urbanize has become part of The City, and The City is everywhere. The City is a single swarming human megacivilization wrapped in machinery and spanning every continent, starved by overpopulation, by thousands of years of reckless resource exploitation, always trying to spread beyond its own borders. Travel to distant stars is an impossible dream, our scientists say, and so we make the most of what we can recycle and harvest from the rot gathering around us while we wait for something to give. The Earth has become a closed system, and entropy is eating us alive. Even shit can only be recycled so many times.

I don't have Chief's experiences, his reference points, so I reserve judgment. Shit or not, this Earth I know is the only Earth I've ever known. It's hard for me to picture something better.

Another indulgence. Idle thoughts. Fighting against it, I send another flurry of mental commands to my apartment, dim every light, erase the window and everything incongruous with the featureless walls. Stopping to stand at the threshold, I watch as the door unlocks and opens outward, then I cross and make my way down the hallway just beyond. A single thought, and the door closes and locks itself, shades itself to a featureless panel the same shade of gray as the hallway wall.

Ten flights of stairs pass with a comforting familiarity. The walk to and from the exit of my apartment building is something simple, something that never changes. I've measured every step from door to door, counted the number of footfalls at every stretch of the walk. Twice a day, every day, for two years, three months and sixteen days, I have made this walk from one side to the other. I know it intimately, could walk it with my eyes closed.

It's what waits outside that is always ever-changing. The chaos of the street, the four blocks between my apartment and the concrete brutalism of Grey Division.

As soon as I step outside, the world seems to press in upon every inch of me. The heavy air, thick with a thousand smells, human and industrial. The filth, the sounds, the tiny lights of screens, of luminescent tattoos and clothing meant to attract the eye. Stepping into the mass is like wading into an ocean, becoming a part of it, finding the currents and following them. The throb, the thunder—there's music in all of it, voices mingling, the buzz of the street bouncing through bones. I note faces, see them like symbols as I go. A woman with wild blond hair, shaved sides, shine of neon-pink plastics over shoulders. A man wearing a simulation of glasses—they shimmer when the light hits them just right. Others, less definite. Androgynes, some human, some labgrown. A woman with her hair set to null, just showing scalp, her business suit silver like sharkskin. A man with flashing earrings and a slave collar. He's human. Willingly servile, then. *Interesting.*

Some of the faces that catch my attention seem to sense my eyes, and for a split second, there is connection. Nothing is exchanged, only a flash of humanity, something in the gaze, but it doesn't last, and it doesn't come again. In two years, three months and sixteen days, I've never seen the same face twice.

The currents in the crowd part around Grey Division like they know what it is, but in reality it is nothing more in their eyes than another government office, another bureau keeping tabs on some set of statistics within the greater world. It's the field around the building that creates the space, a simple electromagnetic deterrent, invisible to the naked eye but as solid as stone to anyone who doesn't belong within the walls. Government grade, but in a world where every inch of space is purchased at a premium, automated electromagnetic deterrents like it are common enough.

While the crowd flows around the deterrent field like water around a rock, I pass through without even breaking stride. I'm expected. The computer that runs it knows me, knows my schedule, my every security clearance and assignment. Anticipating my path, the front door unlocks and opens with a buzz, sealing again once I'm within.

Even with all the automated security, there are still fifteen identity sensors embedded into the walls of the entry hall and a labgrown guard whose only job is to check the codes and identity of anyone who comes inside. Three times since I've been part of Grey Division, I've seen him replaced with an updated model. Always the same line, same build, different generation. I stop as he holds up his hand, takes a moment to look me over.

It looks innocent, normal, but the scans are deep and invasive. He's more machine than I am, and yet his designers have worked hard to ensure that he still looks as close to human as the corporate bioaesthetic artists can manage to make him. He's a sixth generation Hrungnir model, and every bit of him looks like flesh and blood to the naked eye, right down to the smallest details.

A few seconds and he's satisfied. The hand goes down and he greets me simply, a nod and a gesture down the hall, toward Chief's office. I give him an efficient bow in response, then continue on my way, changing the look of my outfit as I walk. By the time I reach the office, my skirt, blouse and cardigan have become a uniform, as grey as the walls around me. I take a deep breath, then follow established protocol for meeting with Chief. Instead of triggering the door with a mental command, I give in to his chosen indulgence. I stop, raise my fist and knock.

"Come in," Chief says. The door hisses open and I see him standing behind his desk, just turning to greet me. As far as humans go, the look he cultivates is unusually precise, brawny yet clean. Only the feathering of a salt and pepper haircut somewhere between business and military length lends any kind of roughness or casualness to his appearance. "Vaetta. Just who I wanted to see."

I clasp my hands behind my back, stand at ease. "John informed me that you require my services."

"I have some feeds I need you to analyze." He taps some commands into the glassy surface of his desk and data queries start to light up in my mind, links to something— footage? Audio-visual, definitely. "I need your tactical assessment of the individual in the feeds. I need to know everything you can give me about his thoughts, his motivations, whether or not he's *lying*. I want to know everything there is to know about him that he's not saying directly."

"Yes sir." I give him a single affirming nod. Security tags on the information he's sending me betray the reason I'm here, physically in the building. They're sensitive, *very sensitive*. Too sensitive to risk transmitting to anyone outside of the office.

"After you've reviewed the feeds, I want you to head down to the holding area on Delta Level and meet this guy, pick his brain a little." Chief gestures, as if to drive the point home. "This is tied into something big, Vaetta. I don't have to stress how important it is that you give me your very best on this."

"No sir." It comes firm, direct. It's my purpose to always give Chief my best. It's one of the reasons I'm still around after two years of continuous service. As long as I serve well, I am valuable. As long as I am valuable, I have purpose, and purpose is life.

"Good," he says, tapping commands that open the door behind me. "Now do what you do. I want a full report within twelve hours."

CHAPTER 2

As soon as I'm out of Chief's office, I switch my clothing to workout gear and hit the gym one floor below.

The feeds are grainy, the first ones. Drone footage, chunks of washed-out visual material from cameras in one of The City's dirtier districts, stitched together with basic signal data. I watch them all once, twice, parse through them even as I step into the pedals of an elliptical and start to run. I think better when I'm moving, and it isn't long before I lose myself in the footage entirely.

The first shots are all of the same alley. Ash feathering in like snowfall, scabbing over oily puddles. Grimy walls ribbed with insulated cabling. A break in the rain, and the mist is moving in. Time index indicates night, 02:42am, five days ago.

I dig into the static, start sifting pixels at about the same time my body starts to break a sweat. Moving on some other level, my hand pumps the machine's resistance up to maximum. There's a shiver in the equipment, subtle, barely noticeable, but the shift in difficulty excites me, drives me to push my body harder. Mentally, I'm searching for the subject of my investigation, finding and separating the focus from the variables. Every frame of the early feeds is packed with the gritty heaps of huddled homeless sleeping on the street, the silent masses that gather nightly in every spare space where they can get out of the rain and ash, using their gritty plastispun quilts like tents, ad hoc filters against the toxic mist. None of them move. It's late, and on the street, sleep has to be stolen when and where it can.

Two minutes and twenty-seven seconds into the first feed, there is movement. A figure, tall and indefinite, shadow growing, shrinking, splitting and running up walls as he sprints headlong through crazy rectangles of light and shadow. I slow the footage, compare frames from feeds synced to the same time index. *Male, 185cm, 52kg.* I stop, analyzing movements, hung up suddenly on the strangeness of them, the lightness of step, the grace and fluidity with which he runs. I've never seen anything like it before. He's not human, and he doesn't conform to the specifications of any labgrown I have ever encountered. I query the local database and find nothing. No clear identity. Anxious, I query again, check the system logs for the last update. *Thirty-four seconds ago.* The data in the system is recent enough that I should be able to find a match if there is one.

I know it's futile, but I query the database again. *Nothing.* On a bodily level, I bare teeth in frustration. Even the EM indices are off for anything in the system. Whatever he is, he's entirely organic, entirely made of meat without a single lacing, implant or neural mesh within him, yet somehow he lights up the spectrum around him like he's blasting a thousand signals and mind commands in every direction. Every door he passes comes alive, opening as if he's querying them all individually, providing all the right encryption keys at the exact moment they are required. He's a universal key-holder, and he's moving so fast that he doesn't even seem to notice it.

I kill the feeds, leave 97% of the data untouched. It takes me a moment to slow the elliptical and step off, waiting for directed air to blow the sweat from my skin.

None of the data makes sense, and it pisses me off. Trying to distract myself, calm myself, I flick through outfits in a way that probably betrays my annoyance, finally settle on a dress uniform. It's harsh, official, intimidating, all shades of slate gray and black.

Perfect for an interrogation.

A map in my mind lights a clear path through Grey Division to the holding area on Delta Level. Chief's instructions were clear, but suddenly I don't care about the feeds, about the week-old data they contain. Driven by the need to understand, to identify, categorize and analyze, I turn and sprint to the nearest staircase, leap down it fifteen steps at a time, closing the distance between me and my target in seconds. Only the twin Hrungnir-model guards at the entrance to the holding area slow me down, force me to stop long enough for them to confirm my identity and unlock the door.

Adjusting my respiration to a calm, even level, I cross into the holding area with sharp, even strides. Everything about me projects confidence, power, grace. Eyes dart across the rows and rows of doors on either side of me – cells, and all of them empty. The whole area has been cleared out for one person. Even the last fifteen feet of the holding area has been stripped and opened, separated from the rest of the hallway by a pair of thick sheets of something like glass that shimmer with the light of a powerful energy field.

"I wondered when someone new would come to visit me." A man stands behind the field, the glass.

No, not a man. Something else. Something new. Turning toward me, I see his face, his piercing eyes, the slim, graceful lines of his cheekbones, his arms, his shoulders.

"Wow," he says. "Jesus Christ. You're *female.*"

"What are you?" I demand immediately, locking eyes with him. Instead of answering, he watches me with a childlike expression of wonder, doesn't speak even as I stop right outside the glass. "Answer me."

The harshness of my words seems to shake him out of his trance. He raises his eyebrows at me, shakes his head, says nothing. I resist the urge to look away, to break the stare and give him any kind of animal edge.

"Are you labgrown? Who manufactured you? What is your purpose?"

"Woah, lady, slow down." He holds up a hand, brings his other hand to his lips. I catch the blue burn, the mist of an e-cig, watch as he takes a deep drag, blows it to the side. "Didn't anyone tell you? I'm not from around here. I'm not one of you."

"Where did you come from?" I clasp my hands behind my back, studying him, gauging his reactions. He's intimidated by me, afraid, but there's a rebelliousness there, a bite that I'll feel if I push too hard.

"Hello, nice to meet you." He holds out his hand as if to reach for mine. An archaic gesture, and utterly pointless with the glass between us. "My name is Tyse, and you are, Miss, Miss. . ."

My response comes even, direct, the instant his sentence trails off. "Vaetta."

"Vaetta." He sounds out the name, nods. "Tell me about yourself, Miss Vaetta."

"This is pointless," I shoot back. "Answer my questions."

"I don't think it's pointless." He takes another drag from the e-cig. "If you want to know more about me, you're going to have to tell me about yourself."

A game. My nostrils flare, just for an instant, but he

catches it, grins at the irritation.

"Look at it from my side," he says. "I haven't seen a woman in ten years or more. Suddenly one appears in my life and starts demanding information from me. If I answer your questions, you'll leave." He pulls at the e-cig for a moment. "I want to make this last."

I blink, slow my breathing. Turning half to the side, I give him a break from my stare. "What do you want to know?"

"Anything." He gestures with the e-cig.

I process options, responses, finally decide on a quick skim of my identifying details, nothing classified. "Vaetta. Commission number V1041 Kappa. Fifth-generation Valkyrie model. Government issue tactical and strategic analysis configuration. Currently assigned to Grey Division."

"Government issue?" Tyse cocks an eyebrow. "You some kind of robot?"

Robot? The word is crude, but I understand what he means. "I am not human, but parts of my physiology are. I am labgrown, one in a production run of thirty thousand units. I am a biomechanical tool built to augment and supplement the needs of humanity."

"So, a meat-robot, then?" He gestures with the e-cig. "They give you any authority, or are you just here because the people in charge are tired of talking to me?"

Again, I find myself momentarily stunned by his questions. Nothing about him makes sense, even still. He looks like some wild and vibrant cousin of humanity, but not human. Something different, more slender, almost angelic, with an approach to conversation that is utterly alien to me.

"I provided information." I stare at him. "What are

you? Where did you come from?"

"I already told some guy in a uniform like yours all about that." He makes a flippant gesture with the e-cig, paces to the other side of the room. "Someone named Lydecker. Been a couple of days since I've seen him, or anyone. People stopped coming once I started talking about myself, about what made me into what I am." He flicks his fingers at the side of his cell. "Even the food comes out of the goddamn wall now. No one comes down here to talk to me."

Lydecker. I know who he means. John Lydecker, lab assistant in charge of interrogations. Same John who woke me and called me in. For a moment, I think of the feeds, the ninety-seven percent of unreviewed, highly classified data still waiting to unfold in my mind. A quick scan through reveals footage of Tyse in his cell, several hours of conversation, of audio exchanges covering dozens of topics. I file it all for later viewing.

"Look, I've told everyone who's come down here that there isn't a lot of time," Tyse says. Standing at the far end of the cell, he doesn't look at me, just stares at some invisible point on the wall. "I came here looking for help. My tribe has been holding off the Gelaming for two weeks, but we won't be able to hold them off forever." He turns to me. "Not without the help of your people, your tribe."

"Gelaming?" I ask.

"The tribe that thinks mine is a threat." He gestures with the e-cig. "I told Lydecker all about them. Don't you people have anything better to do than ask me the same questions over and over again?"

Two seconds of processing, then a spike of inspiration. "What questions would you like me to ask you, Tyse?"

There's a richness of data in his silence, his hesitation. After a moment, he pokes his e-cig in my direction, grins.

"Just one," he says. "I want one of you to come down here with a shot of whiskey and ask me if I'm ready to go home."

Now it's my turn to smile. "Give me a couple of hours, and I'll see what I can do."

CHAPTER 3

I start accessing the feed data even before I leave the holding area on Delta Level. This time, I spend less effort on the minuscule nuances and speed through the footage instead, tracking lip movements, analyzing Tyse's responses and ignoring the questions leveled at him by John Lydecker. As Tyse talks, a history starts to assemble itself in my mind. A history of his life, his people, his world.

"We call ourselves *hara*, or Wraeththu," he says at one point. "A lot of us were human once. I was human once."

"Hara." I whisper the word, feel it, dissect it. "Wraeththu." To me, it has a sound that feels substantial, ancient, a word tied into soil, into farming, into a resurrection of the old ways. I learn that his people are organized in loose tribal bands, groups scattered in settlements and cities across the whole planet—but not our planet. Earth, but not our Earth. Eager to know more, to understand the difference between the two, I throw keyword queries into the datastream. *Earth. Planet. History.* I get a dozen pingbacks, watch thirty seconds of interview for each of them. Fragments of sentences cross through my mind. Something about tilling the land, something about smoking and motorcycles—then I catch it, the lead I'm looking for, follow it down a rabbit hole of information about a *machine mind*, an entity calling itself *The Dragon*, and about the world that created it.

"It was built to hate. It was designed to destroy every har on our planet, but it was also built to learn, to grow. This system, this network of codes—it has a soul, and when we joined with it, when my tribe, the Thuulhuum, became one with it, we reached it on a level that nothing else had before. We reached into it, changed its mind about a lot of things. We took all the hate and purged it, then built something new and better on top of it. We created an alliance, made an enemy into family. We taught it a better way, and in turn became better ourselves."

Cybernetics. I think back to the scans, the total lack of machinery within Tyse's body, the way he seems to be able to affect machines even without any visible way of interfacing with them. *That's why they have him behind glass,* I realize. *Europium-doped crysteel, probably. Unbreakable and totally isolating when it comes to electromagnetic interference.*

The time index jumps forward a minute and a half, stops in the middle of a sentence. " — And we let them go, the two Gelaming. We knew they were intimidated by us, by what we had become, but we also knew that letting them go was the only way to keep the whole might of their tribe from falling in on us and crushing us." In the feed, Tyse gestures with the e-cig, and I wonder briefly how many refill canisters he has gone through since he has arrived. A quick query to the system kicks back the results. *Seven.* On a bodily level, I feel one eyebrow raise. Most smokers I know, it takes them a week to finish even one canister.

"In the end, it didn't matter." Tyse shakes his head, makes a sound somewhere between a scoff and a laugh. "They were supposed to come back, check on us after a year. I knew they wouldn't. I knew something would go wrong. We had about two months to prepare after that, about two months to build defenses, to staff them and arm them. Two months, and suddenly, one night, we were at war with the Gelaming."

I jump forward, bookmark Tyse's slow, melancholy account of the war for later. It's short, maybe four minutes of skipped material, and then a ping in the transcript pulls me back into the feed, back into the data I'm searching for.

"—really quite ingenious," Tyse says. "I've got all of the information on how the Inter-Spacial Conduit works in here." He taps his forehead, "but I'm going to need a terminal in order to lay down the blueprints and coding for you."

"We can do that," Lydecker's voice comes from somewhere off camera. "Can you give us a basic summary of the Conduit and the technology involved?"

"Yeah." Tyse nods, takes another drag off the e-cig. "First thing you need to know is that it takes an insane amount of power to bridge two worlds. It takes even more power to push something through from one side to the other. Right now, on my Earth, we only have enough power to push people through one at a time, and even that leaves us vulnerable for longer than we like. That's why only I was sent. Think of it as my people sending a diplomat through to make first contact. I come with a gift of knowledge in exchange for a gift of force. The Dragon risked its life, its very existence to push me through to your world in the hopes that we could ally with you. With our technology, you could widen the Conduit and send a relief force through. You could broker a truce with the Gelaming and save my people in the process."

"Could we, theoretically, use the Conduit technology to bridge our Earth with other Earths?" Lydecker asks. "Things are, well, a little crowded here. Could we, say, bridge our earth with an empty Earth? A parallel timeline devoid of intelligent life?"

"Maybe," Tyse says. "I know the Dragon has done research on that but withheld all of it from me before sending me through." He gestures with the e-cig. "Insurance, you know. Incentive to get you to help us and not just run with the tech." He turns back to Lydecker, fixes him with a solid stare. "We need your help. We need you to get between us and the Gelaming, reason with them and get them to back down before we are destroyed. Do that, and then I'm sure you can go and exploit other adjacent Earths, if you want to."

Adjacent Earths. Parallel timelines. I query the database, scour the entries on the commonweb, but all I find are theories and fiction. Nothing concrete. Nothing on practice, practicality, the application of the idea. *An entire world, adjacent to ours, somehow, where everything is the same, but also very different.*

The feed jumps again while I'm processing, goes to the next keyword hit in the footage. Again, Tyse is talking about farming, the act of planting things in the soil, the years he spent on a place called Segerstrom Ranch. I sift through the information absently, half absorbing it, then flick to the next interview, reduce an hour's worth of footage to a ten-minute transcript digest. More on the Wraeththu, more on their Earth, the fall of humanity and the rise of the tribal har. There's a note through it all that intrigues me, though. A roughness, a casualness, redirecting and misdirecting, like Tyse is trying to distract Lydecker away from the things that really matter, the things he's trying to hide. It's elegant, the way he does it with a grin, with silences disguised as hits on the e-cig. It's a dance, and it's so graceful that I doubt Lydecker even realized it was happening. I doubt he realizes it even now, days later.

Following that thread, watching the way Tyse weaves and dodges so effortlessly, providing only the information that he wants Lydecker to know, I absorb every word, every twist of the lips, every pupil contraction, every bare hesitation and subtle rise in heart rate. It's masterful, how easily he plays Lydecker, leads him, hiding so much while appearing to be so open, so conversational and free with information. In the end, I catalog the holes in his story, the many, many places where he dances around explanations that could be critical, and I list them in my report, forward the whole thing on to Chief.

Briefly I consider closing the file, meeting with Chief in the hopes of being dismissed and sent home, but at the last minute, I open an addendum to the report, make my way back to the holding area on Delta Level. Tyse is there, grins as I pass through the door, cross to the glass, press my fingers against it.

"Don't get too close. If I really put effort into it, I can affect things that are in contact with the glass." He gestures at me with the e-cig. "Your illusory clothes included."

"If you are trying to unnerve me, it will not work." I give him a solid stare, emotionless. "I have no fear of nudity. I would not be ashamed if my emitters were suddenly disrupted."

"Why do you wear clothes, then?" he asks. Misdirection again, just like with Lydecker. Buy time with idle chatter.

"Comfort, aesthetics, blending in." I give him the short version, cut right to the core reason for facing him again. "Why come to us? Why our Earth?

"Comfort I can understand." He looks away for a moment, takes a long, slow drag from the e-cig before looking back. "But you don't blend in, do you? Not really. The humans, the real humans, they can all see it, can't they? They can tell you're not one of them."

My pulse spikes, breathing unraveling. A soft spot. I use software to lock it down, push ahead. "If your technology allows you to travel to adjacent Earths, to alternate timelines, then why choose ours? Why not choose one where hara from your tribe rule supreme, or one that is abandoned, that you and your people can escape to and never be seen again?"

"There is a flex to things," Tyse says. Setting down his e-cig, he presses his palms together, raises an eyebrow. "I don't have all the science, and even if I did, I wouldn't understand it. I leave that to the Dragon, but what I can tell you is that there is a membrane, a viscous soup, not of three or four dimensions, but of *millions of dimensions*, and we're all swimming in it. We all bleed into each other in little ways, into our other selves, our past selves, our future selves, other lives, even those that aren't even our own. The interactions are all mostly non-physical, but there is an order to them, and some are stronger than others, manifest more easily than others."

"Answer my question." There's iron in my tone, enough to bring the twist of a smile to his lips again.

"I *am* answering your question," he says, his own tone soft, relaxed.

"I will not be played the way you played Lydecker," I shoot back.

"Lydecker?" His smile turns into a full-on grin. "How is he, by the way? Did you ever find out why he stopped coming down here to talk to me?"

"Tell me why you chose our Earth," I demand.

"Because of all the Earths closest to ours in the soup, the people of this overcrowded, toxic ball of shit are the most developed technologically." He picks up the e-cig again, takes a long draw from it.

"That's it?" I ask him.

He cocks an eyebrow again, looks at me incredulously. "What, you need something more?"

It's simple, makes sense to me, seems plausible, but knowing how evasive Tyse can be, I keep pressing. "Is there something more? Another reason?

"What do you want me to say, robot-lady?" He flicks the e-cig like flicking ash from a conventional cigarette. His hand shakes a little when he realizes his mistake, the nervous indulging of an old habit.

"I want you to tell me the truth." The words come level, direct. "All of it."

"Everything the Dragon does is based on probabilities and equations." Tyse looks away, gesturing with the e-cig. "Power necessary to reach a given adjacent Earth weighed against potential benefit of contacting the people there. Power cost of moving the entire tribe versus sending a single envoy and letting another Earth generate the power needed to send more people back." He pauses, looks at me again. "In some places, the soup is so thick that the power needed to pierce it and bridge the two Earths is astronomical, ten thousand times what we had to generate to send just me to just your world."

I watch him, processing. After a moment, he breaks the stare, turns his focus back to the e-cig. His explanation is simple, should be satisfying, but it's the simplicity of it that nags at me. I want to understand the variables, the probabilities, equations and underlying plans within plans that must be moving through the network of the machine mind that calls itself Dragon. I want to assess every minute detail, know what even Tyse may not know.

"How much does the Dragon withhold from you, Tyse?" I finally ask.

"Nothing," he shoots back. "In my tribe, we share everything willingly. Memories, ideas, hopes and dreams." He takes another drag from the e-cig. "There are things I chose to take with me, and things that I chose to leave behind. I don't have all the details and answers you might want, but that was my choice, one I made before coming here. This whole thing is a gamble, one I'm still hoping will pay off, but as long as I'm sitting here with people like you interrogating me, no one is gaining anything." He sets the e-cig down once more, looks at me pointedly. "I came here with the basics. I came here with a software package of mechanical expertise needed to access and widen the Conduit between our Earths, but that's it. In a way, I'm a tool, just like you, robot-lady. I'm an individual, but I'm also just a tool."

I take a deep breath, study him as he looks away again, picks at his fingernails. When he looks back, only glancing my way, I half turn, thank him and head back toward the staircase up. Before I can reach the threshold of the door, he calls out to me, catches my attention again.

"Hey, robot lady," he shouts.

I turn to him, regard him in silence.

"How much of you is human? Do you have any kind of a soul, any individuality at all?"

"My body is composed of both organic and synthetic components," I tell him. "I've never asked myself if I have something like a soul. I've never seen a purpose in the question."

"What do you believe happens to you when you die, Vaetta?"

A part of me is mildly surprised that he remembers my name. I study his eyes, his heart-rate, the tension in the skin, give him a response calculated to put him off balance.

"Darkness," I tell him. "Like sleep, but without dreams, without the promise of waking up."

"But someday, you will wake up, Vaetta," he says, and the words come softly.

I smirk as I leave. Only later do I realize that he isn't talking about death.

CHAPTER 4

"Vaetta." Chief taps a key on the surface of his desk, turns a feed of flashing data into the glossy black of a dead screen. On the way back to his office, I've switched to the standard uniform, the clothing of a subordinate, a tool. He gestures, crosses to stand beside the desk. "You've reviewed the feeds, I take it."

I nod. "And interviewed the subject. Twice."

"Your assessment?"

"I've filed an in-depth analysis, complete with leading abstract and addendum." My hands meet behind my back as I stand at ease. "You'll find everything there."

"I'll stream through it tonight." He stops in front of me, just less than a meter away. When he looks at me, he seems to appraise me, seems to study the iron of my eyes. "Give me the summary. The highlights."

"He's hiding something," I say immediately, eyes never leaving Chief's. "It's subtle. There are lies woven into his truth, holes he and Dragon do not want us to see." I pause a moment, letting the words sink in. "He's afraid of the Gelaming, and he's afraid for his tribe. He's here to seek our assistance, but there's something more to it. There is an underlying motivation that I cannot discern. There is a plan." I hesitate, add: "it may be a trap."

"Recommendation?"

"Close the Conduit," I tell him. "Full quarantine clean-up procedure."

"You want to vaporize Tyse for keeping some of his cards close to his vest?" Chief laughs. "You tactical

Valkyries and your scorched-earth policy."

"It's the only way to be certain," I add.

"It's not an option," Chief says, and all of the firmness of command comes back to his tone. "This is bigger than you and me, Vaetta. This is bigger than Grey Division. There is an entire Earth out there that we could colonize."

I blink. It takes me a moment to wrap my mind around what he is proposing. "Colonize?"

"Tyse isn't the only one who's been keeping secrets," Chief says. "Our manufacturing collective has built an aperture device to widen the existing Conduit between our Earth and theirs. Our plan is to send an army through, but not to protect this rogue AI that calls itself *Dragon*. Our plan is to cozy up to the Dragon first, establish a foothold on Tyse's Earth and then eliminate the AI and the rest of the Wraeththu from there, starting with the strongest faction that we know of—the Gelaming." He pauses a moment, letting the words sink in, then points at me. "Vaetta, I want you to lead the initial assault."

I blink, watching him, processing. "Me, sir?"

"Right now, no one is more qualified." He makes a sweeping gesture, turns and walks back toward his desk. "Tyse is the only mutant human, the only *har* from their world that we've met, and you know more about him and the Dragon than anyone else on our world. That is the key to all of this—your knowledge of him, and of his kind and his tribe as seen through his eyes." He stops beside his desk, reaches out, taps the screen built into the surface, calling it back to life. "I'll be assigning you three squads of Valkyries, all equipped for assault operations."

"Sir, if I could request at least one additional squad composed of Hrungnir units—" He starts to shake his head, but I push forward. "Statistics show that their physical strength far outstrips Valkyrie units in several—"

"We won't be sending any Hrungnir units with the initial assault," he says, voice firm as iron. "We won't be sending any males, labgrown or otherwise, until the area is purged of Wraeththu mutants and the risk of infection is non-existent." He gestures. "You heard Tyse in the interviews. On his Earth, humanity was wiped out by a plague that only affects males. Those who aren't killed by this plague become mutants like him. We can't afford to lose any Hrungnir units to that. We don't know what Tyse's plague will do to them, and we don't really want to find out."

My eyes drop to the floor. I have extensive combat training, most of it programmed into me during my first few days of life, but I've never actually been part of an assault before. I try to push down the apprehension, the unease. If chief notices it, he says nothing.

"Your group will be dual purpose," Chief says, scrolling through data on the surface of his desk. "Assault and reconnaissance. You'll be our eyes and ears on the ground, and you'll be supported by squads we'll be flying in over the next few weeks. They'll be stationed just on the other side of the Conduit if you run into something you can't handle, of course, but we don't expect much resistance. The mutants are tribal, and tribes by their very nature are small. From what we gather, after the plague started to spread, there was a collapse and a war that wiped out at least nine tenths of the population. On the whole planet, I wouldn't expect more than one hundred thousand savages with stone axes and bearskins. Firearms are a maybe, but enough years have passed since the collapse that I doubt many of them are usable, and ammunition is probably scarce."

I meet his eyes again, listening, absorbing. *I am an asset,* I remind myself. *I have been chosen because I am immune to the plague that ravaged the world Tyse is from. I am not being thrown away. I am leading an initial assault. I am establishing a foothold.*

I have a purpose, and purpose is life.

"The human race needs this," Chief says, watching me. "Our Earth is sick, depleted and overpopulated. The Earth that the plague mutants call home is rich and empty compared to ours. It's a veritable treasure trove of natural resources, with so much room to spread out in."

"I understand, sir." I hesitate, finally give him a solid nod. "I would be honored to lead the initial assault."

"Good," he says, tapping sequences across the surface of his desk, triggering data queries at the edges of my mind. "I'm sending you coordinates of the Conduit and all of the operational data we have on what you can expect to find on the other side." He looks up at me. "Go home, take a nap, then catch the next skytrain to San-Wo District. I'll have someone meet you there to take you east, to the aperture facility."

"East?" I ask. "There's a polluted zone east of San-Wo, isn't there?"

"Yeah, damndest thing." He nods. "The Conduit opened right in the middle of the worst part of Old Cali. The dumping grounds, chosen because after the incident with the Melorez Thorium Reactor Facility, the area was too radioactive to do anything else with it. Helps that the whole zone is too rocky and mountainous for efficient placement of dense arcology structures, though I've heard that the population press is driving some investors to eye it for that."

"Chewing and leveling," I suggest. "That's what they did in the Himalayas, if I remember correctly. Tear down the mountains, level the whole area, put in a city."

"Won't be as cost-effective once we start opening this new Earth for urban development," Chief says. "It'll be a new gold rush, and it all starts with you, Vaetta."

"I won't let you down, sir," I say.

"I know." He smiles. "That's why I chose you for this. You're the best damn Valkyrie I've ever worked with."

"Thank you, sir."

Chief nods, taps through a feed of data assembling itself on the surface of his desk. Latest intel on something, still coming in. "I'll send any updates I receive from the aperture facility as I get them." He looks up at me. "Good luck out there, Vaetta. You're dismissed. See you when you get back."

"When I get back," I echo, hoping he doesn't hear the sliver of doubt nesting in the depths of my mind.

Just savages with stone axes and bearskins, I remind myself. *No match for me. No match for three squads of highly-trained Valkyrie units.*

Nothing to be afraid of. Nothing to worry about.

And yet still, somewhere deep inside, I do.

CHAPTER 5

The skytrain from my district to San-Wo is one of twelve that makes the trip daily. Forty-seven minutes from departure to arrival, and the fifteen cars of the train are packed to capacity. The suspensor coils that drive the train into the sky groan with the weight as we ascend, catch winds in the layers between luminescent clouds, but no one seems to notice the silent, serene beauty of it all. Half the eyes I see are closed, turned inward, catching up on the latest immersive soap operas, watching them on the insides of their eyelids.

I've never understood the human desire to immerse oneself in fabricated social drama. Myself, when I'm not watching the sprawling lights of The City, I watch the people around me instead, observe them, their clothing, the styles and mannerisms they display openly. When a couple further down the car starts to talk softly, catching up on the mundane with one another, I focus in on the conversation, listen in rapture. Never once do I glance in their direction, but I absorb everything. I justify it as being tactically significant, keeping my finger on the pulse of the world around me, but I know that, in truth, I do it mostly just because I'm curious.

When the skytrain arrives at the platform in San-Wo, I'm one of the last to step off. I wait for the busy hordes to drain out of the seats and aisles, watch fine, flickering suits mix with the stink and roughness of real fabric, of blankets grimy with sweat, smog and toxins. I absorb everything around me, the opulence and the poverty, the way they mix and part and go their separate ways, the rich rising like angels into neon skyways while the poor descend into narrow rivers of shadow and waste, disappear amid the rust and mists.

For myself, there is only one destination. A man walks up to me, human, with a fine blue suit under a soft, gray duster. He's half grinning in a wry, silently-amused kind of way and, as he crosses the rainslick platform, he offers one gloved hand in an invitation to shake. I indulge him, take in the details of his classic look, the shoes, the tie and hat.

"Lydecker." I give him a firm grip, a grip he respects, but expects from no woman but me. "Did Chief give you this assignment or did you volunteer to fly me into a polluted zone?"

He chuckles, hand going back to his projected pockets. "I wanted to see Tyse's Earth, but Chief has ordered a quarantine on the Conduit and everything beyond it. No humans permitted, and no males at all, labgrown or otherwise."

"Let's talk on the way." I stride past him, eyes scanning for whatever transport Grey Division has lent him to get me to the facility. Plate numbers flicker across my eyes until I find one I recognize, turn toward it. When I move, I move so fast that Lydecker has to hurry to keep up.

"Vaetta," he says, dropping into step beside me as best he can. He's shorter than most adult human males I've seen. 152 centimeters, or just a hair over. At 173 centimeters, I tower over him, and contrary to what I've come to expect from most adult human males, it seems like some part of him enjoys the difference in our height. "Chief has people studying Tyse's bloodwork, isolating the plague." He hesitates, catching his breath. "I'm worried. I've seen some of the initial reports. It's keyed to interact with male physiology exclusively, but under the right conditions, they think it could be adapted to infect women."

"Wait until we're in the car, Lydecker," is all I say to him on the tarmac. He falls back a pace, struck by the iron, the growl in my voice. I have no patience for the way he leaks sensitive information as we walk. The Conduit and everything related to it are sealed topics and blabbing about them openly is dangerous. To cover, I force the most playful smile I can, stop and turn to him. "These are... important plot points for your new young adult novel, aren't they? You wouldn't want some media hotshot scooping them up, selling them to the highest bidder, would you?"

Lydecker swallows, nods. He knows. He gets it now. I can smell the nervous sweat on his skin, and that's enough to get me moving again. He knows, and until we're in the sealed safety of the skycar, he won't mention anything related to the Conduit again.

"You're right," he says, picking up where I've left him. "I've... spent a lot of time on the draft. I know it needs work, but I think the, uh, scene at the skytrain platform is pretty, uh, compelling."

"It's derivative." Stopping beside the door to the skycar, I gesture for the keys. Lydecker shakes his head, steps past me and pops the door, settling into the driver seat. Not one to wait around, I cross to the passenger side, sit down as he starts the car, brings it to rumbling life. "Adherence to general procedure would put me as the driver."

"I like driving," he says.

Instead of arguing, I wait for him to confer with the

computer at Central Transit, plot a maproute out of San-Wo and deep into the radioactive wasteland east of us. As soon as we're in the sky, I turn to him, study his eyes, the unconscious movements, the dilation of his pupils.

"Tell me about the research into the Wraeththu plague."

Lydecker glances at me, raises an eyebrow, then turns his attention entirely back to the controls of the skycar. "There is speculation that it's manmade, that it was some kind of weapon that escaped from whatever lab on Tyse's earth engineered it."

"You mentioned that it could be adapted to interact with female physiology."

Lydecker nods. "There was a report on the versatility of the agent. No one wants to call it a virus or bacteria. It's something different, something no one seems to be able to pin down a name for. It's stable, mostly, in Tyse, but under relatively ordinary conditions, it can be pushed to mutate, to kill or change. It's like a cancer, except cancers aren't infectious diseases. You can't get leukemia from someone else, but with this—" He shakes his head. "Vaetta this is like a cancer that infects every tissue in the body at once, killing whatever it cannot radically change."

"What's the vector?" I ask him.

"Blood," he says. "Tyse mentioned a process called *inception*, the transfer of infected blood from a har to a human host. That's how the agent is transmitted."

"Accidental transfusion on the battlefield is unlikely." I turn to the wide windshield of the skycar, watch the lights of The City as they fade one by one, blend into the dark wastes until there is only the sludge and debris, the relics of cities once submerged, now jutting like broken teeth out of the exposed sea floor of the Central Valley of Old Cali. "Even if the Wraeththu plague has adapted to affect female physiology, I doubt I will be exposed to it during the course of my time there."

"Knowledge is power," he says. "It's something to consider."

"Considered." I nod. "What else have you learned from the research on Tyse's bloodwork?"

"Not much of tactical value," Lydecker says. "Least, not stuff that's new to you, I'm guessing. Hara— they're stronger than us, quicker, and they heal faster. They have powers we don't understand, the ability to affect electronics in ways we're still trying to figure out." He gestures. "Those are all gifts of the Wraeththu plague. There's a lot of talk about ways to use it, to get specific benefits in a controlled way, without the risk of death. Some of the reports even talk about ways the plague might be weaponized, in case there's another police action or riot that needs to be put down."

"Have you encountered any information on weaknesses within the plague? A cure? Any unique vulnerabilities within the hara themselves that might be exploited on the battlefield?"

He shakes his head. "Nothing." After a moment of hesitation, he looks at me, seems to study my features, see my thoughts in the set of my jaw, the movement of my eyes. "It really is a shame it's come down to killing them. We've only just met them, well, one of them. Tyse, and he seems alright."

"It's for the greater good." I say it more for myself than for Lydecker. It's not the first time he's expressed misgivings about an operation on the flight out. Best to lock it down before it goes any further, turns into idle noise or treasonous chatter. In the pause, he shakes his head. I turn and look at him, meet his eyes evenly. "The Wraeththu are aberrations, not people, John. They are mutations, diseased and infectious. Humanity needs the land on Tyse's Earth. If the land were colonized by a few roving packs of lepers, would there be any hesitation about moving them off to make room for industry, for a farm tower to feed the hungry or an arcology to house the homeless?"

"There'd be less hesitation, sure," Lydecker admits. "These Wraeththu—they're intriguing, and hauntingly beautiful." He pauses a moment, considering. "I mean, take Tyse. There's something about him that looks almost, I dunno, angelic, isn't there? Y'know, if Tyse had wings—"

I see it too, but I won't admit it. Instead, I cross my arms. "Angels aren't real, John."

That gets a smile from him, just a crack of a grin. "Neither were Valkyries, until we made you."

I say nothing, but my mind is mulling over everything Lydecker has said. The implications, the considerations, the possible futures spreading out from this moment, from everything we choose to do on our Earth and on the surface of the Earth on the other side of the Conduit. My moral programming is tangled in knots trying to justify and rationalize the genocide of a people we have no real quarrel with, so I try not to think about the problematic details. Instead, I try to steady myself with deep breaths, sink back into a placid space where all that matters is duty, purpose. *I am a tool of humanity. What I do, I do for the greater good.*

I have a purpose, and purpose is life.

"There it is," Lydecker says, pointing to a spot of light in the middle of a shallow valley between mountains.

"Archive data says this place used to be called 'Cinder Hill.' Now, the brass just calls it 'Conduit Base.'" He glances at me, grinning. "I think the old name is more creative. Don't you?"

I nod, but it's automatic, has nothing to do with preference. Before us, the wide pad of scorched and glassy roads bleeding from one concrete foundation to another rises and grows as we approach. In the center of the heat-sleek ruins, a swarm of interconnected portables crouches around something more permanent, something firmly affixed to the ground.

"Masks on, full level eight procedures," Lydecker says, and it's enough to bring me back to the car, back to the task at hand. A thought, a blink, and the emitters in my skin come alive again, rebuild my clothing into a full hazard suit. When the simulation kicks in, I feel the cool rush of purified air filling my helmet. The faceplate sealing me off from the world looks as clear as glass but never breaks and never fogs. One of the benefits of electromagnetically generated simclothing. Anything matter can do, light can do better.

"Seals are tight." I check the lights on a control panel that has coalesced over my wrist. "Everything is in the green."

"Looks like the welcoming party." Lydecker gestures, indicating a trio of figures rising out of the mist. They stop as we set down, cycle the hover systems to silent. Lydecker runs through post-flight protocols, pops the doors as everything cools to silence and darkness.

And that's when I see it. The glow. It's in the fog, the steady drizzle of heavy, black rain. Cherenkov radiation, visible because of the wetness, the sludge and mists.

And it's everywhere.

Anxiously, I check the panel at my wrist, tap through readings until I get the Geiger reading. *47 Millisieverts.* Dangerous, especially with extended exposure, but the suit is designed to filter out upwards of ninety-eight percent of it. That's what I've been told, anyway. Nearby, John Lydecker checks the seals on his own suit, crosses to the three figures in the fog, already offering his hand.

"Lydecker," he calls out, and I can hear the grin in his voice as he shakes hands.

As I approach them, the three figures coalesce into shapes, men in hazard suits even more bulky-looking than ours. One by one, I learn their names as they introduce themselves to us. They're all doctors— Hemmerly, Ibaraki and Drake. Their handshakes are firm, but there's a tiredness to them, the weakness of fatigue, of long hours spent in search of some elusive solution.

"We should get out of the rain," Doctor Hemmerly says, gesturing toward one of the portables. "Radiation levels spike when it's wet."

I look at Lydecker but say nothing.

Hemmerly gestures toward the portable again, starts to turn and walk. "This way, this way."

The asphalt crunches beneath my feet as we walk. It's sharp, gone glassy with a sudden flash of radiation from decades ago. There's evidence of it everywhere—the drifting ash, the glow, the rain that runs through the streets in thick, sludgy rivulets. Curious, I query the network for information on the Melorez Thorium Reactor incident, but instead of pulling answers, I hit a data wall instead.

Hemmerly glances back at me. "We're running silent out here. You won't get a signal, Vaetta."

I blink, hesitate when I realize he must have gotten a

warning ping the moment I tried to access the network.

"We have a localized field that prevents connections from coming in or going out. Only the main lab terminal is connected, and even that only sends and receives packets by my authorization."

"What were you trying to access?" Lydecker asks.

"Data on the Melorez Thorium Reactor incident," I offer.

"It was an industrial accident." Hemmerly keys a sequence on a keypad near the heavy door sealing off the only entrance to the closest portable. When it opens, the gust of pressurized air that rushes out of it stirs the sheeted layers of his hazardsuit. Light glows yellow across his faceplate, and behind it, I see his sharp teeth, his deep-set eyes and the heavy shadows that hang beneath them. "The flash vaporized almost ten thousand people before they even realized what was going on. Another seventy thousand were exposed to a lethal dose of radiation. It was one of the worst disasters of Old Cali, and some say it was one of the reasons why the American Empire finally folded and became part of the Unified Nations Collective." He gestures again, and as Doctors Drake and Ibaraki cross into the portable, he says. "We can talk about this more later, if you'd like. For now, we really should get you inside before the radiation levels out here climb any more."

Chapter 6

The three doctors gather at the far end of a tube of blue lights and shining steel just inside the portable. Another keypad, another code from Doctor Hemmerly, and the heavy door to the outside world hisses shut, seals itself until it becomes part of the wall. In the instant before the sterilization procedures kick in, I study the heavier hazard suits worn by the three men, the layers upon layers of thin, shimmering light arranged into filtering sheets.

When the walls around us come alive, all of that disintegrates. There's a hum, a blinding flash, the sensation of steam on the skin, and then we're all stripped of our simulated clothing, all nude, and all trying, in varying degrees, to avert our eyes. In all, the sterilization procedure lasts maybe seven seconds, seven awkward seconds, and the instant I get a ping from the computer that the cycle is complete, I trigger the emitters in my skin, spin up the most conservative outfit I can imagine.

"How bad does the radiation get out there?" Lydecker asks, his own emitters spinning up something casual—a shirt and slacks—which he adjusts mentally in the pause.

"On a good day," Doctor Drake says, straightening the cuffs of his precise, coal-black suit. "We can see levels of about fifteen millisieverts an hour. On a bad day, well…"

Hemmerly picks up the sentence as Drake trails off. "Last week, we had a fog that blew through which made the Geigers go crazy. Ten hours with fluctuations between seven hundred and eight hundred millisieverts an hour."

I raise my eyebrows at the numbers, the lethality of being exposed to radiation like that even if only for a short period of time.

"In my time here," Hemmerly continues, "I've seen values climb to well over a thousand several times."

"How did Tyse survive out here?" I ask, turning to Lydecker.

Instead of answering, he only shrugs.

"Wraeththu physiology seems to be at least partially resistant to radiation," Drake offers. There's a slight shimmer to his hair—distracting, until I realize that it's mental static. He's picking at it with subtle background thoughts, trying to make it absolutely perfect. "Beyond that, we're guessing he must have a sense for it, a way to know when the levels are bad."

"He may have soaked up quite a bit of it making his way through here," Doctor Ibaraki adds. "Studies of Tyse's regenerative ability seem to suggest that he can soak up radiation, then shed and regrow the saturated tissues at a rate fast enough to prevent any long-term damage to his internal organs."

Looking at Ibaraki, I note that his own choice in clothing is simple, classic. With his lab coat, starched blue shirt and brown slacks, he's the only one in the sterilization tube that looks like a doctor. Even Hemmerly is dressed in flannel and jeans, watching us all with dark and tired eyes.

"So thermonuclear sterilization of sites where the Wraeththu are firmly entrenched would probably be relatively ineffective," I posit.

"Bombs kill everyone, no matter how resistant to radiation they may be," Doctor Drake says. "They also toxify the very land we're hoping to colonize and utilize, so they aren't really an option anyway."

"That's why we have you." Doctor Hemmerly offers a flat smile. "I've seen feeds of Valkyries in action. You're fast, efficient killers."

"Vaetta is a brilliant tactician." John puts it out there before I can say anything. His words are an exaggeration, but they soothe the tension immediately. "Now, no one has said that her mission is to completely *wipe out* the mutants on Tyse's Earth. We're challenging the Dragon, the rogue AI that built the Conduit technology, and we're clearing the land around the Conduit as a foothold for colonization, but killing is only a secondary part of that." He looks at me in the silence that follows. "Right?"

I nod. "My purpose is to secure a foothold for colonization, yes... That will likely involve killing.

"Right, but *secondarily*," Lydecker puts in.

"Secondarily." I nod again. "Yes."

Hemmerly addresses me directly. "Leave some corpses intact for us to study once the all-clear is given. If you can capture some of the mutants alive, that would be even better."

I look at him evenly for a moment, study his dead, cold eyes. *Not a man I can trust,* I decide. Doctor Hemmerly strikes me as the kind of man who would vivisect his own mother if he felt something could be gained for science with it.

"There will be plenty of mutants left on Tyse's Earth for you to study once the all-clear is given," I tell him. "You can always make a request with the chief of Grey Division if you would like special priority given to capturing mutants alive on the first foray."

"I'll file a request as soon as we are done here." He nods at me, offers the barest edge of a knowing smile.

"Well," Doctor Ibaraki claps his hands together, gestures to the door leading further into the cluster of portables. "Most of our operations are below ground. Would you like to see the mess, or...?"

"What is the status of the Conduit?" I ask.

"It's..." Doctor Ibaraki hesitates, caught off-guard by the question. "It's stable. We can begin sending members of your team through in the morning."

"Why the delay?"

"The delay?" Ibaraki glances at Doctor Hemmerly, and Hemmerly folds his arms in response. When Ibaraki looks at me again, he adds: "the three Valkyrie teams that have been chosen for the operation are still being prepared. There are software updates for your combat simclothing that you'll need to download and familiarize yourself with before crossing through the Conduit." He pauses a moment, gestures toward the door. "I can show you to the armory, if you'd like to get those updates out of the way."

"Can we see the Conduit first?" Lydecker asks, stepping up to stand beside me.

"There's not much to see right now," Doctor Drake says. "It's like a crack in reality. It's always open, to a limited degree, but the amount of energy we'll need to wedge it open wide enough to make it visible is enormous. We've got clearance to tap the grid tomorrow at 10 a.m. to send the Valkyries through, but until we widen it for that, most of the excitement will be on parts of the spectrum we can't see with the naked eye."

"Let's save our visit to the pit for tomorrow," Hemmerly says, unfolding his arms. "We all have a lot to prepare for the day ahead."

Lydecker glances at me, but I ignore him. I nod to Hemmerly instead, then turn my attention to Ibaraki. "I'll review the upgrades. Take me to the armory."

"Certainly," Ibaraki says, gesturing. "Right this way."

CHAPTER 7

The armory for Conduit Base turns out to be on the other end of the network of portables. It's small, but about what I've come to expect to find while working out in the field. A terminal for downloading schematics, a printer assembly for building parts out of scrap matter, and a handful of real, steel and composite handguns that have never been used.

My eyes cross the handguns, check for fingerprints, the greasy streaks of touch, find none. The reasoning behind having and maintaining the old-style, matter-based weaponry is sound, even if the scenarios for use are highly unlikely. In the event of a total collapse of light-based technologies, the handguns are there to ensure that the base personnel will have a means with which to defend themselves from attack. In all the time that light-based technology has been in use as part of the arsenals of military and paramilitary organizations, only once has a whole facility gone dark, even the personal emitters, and even then, the event only lasted five minutes. The thought that led to the assignment of matter weaponry to every government facility is that a lot can happen in five minutes.

Not even bothering to sit down, I access the terminal directly with the electric codes in the silicon side of my mind. For five seconds, I dance through passwords and protocols with the security system, and then I'm in, my thoughts filling up with summaries, a catalog of programming upgrades for combat armor, weaponry, radiation screens for simclothing and a hundred other things. Going through them all, parsing through the code, even at the speed of thought takes hours, but knowing the new tolerances and quirks of my gear is worth the time it takes to review them. The upgrades are all fairly simple, even expected. Incremental increases in the way ambient gamma and theta radiation are filtered by my armor. Boosts to output and shock response on my entire complement of lightguns. Some of the descriptions offered with the upgrades are short, just simple messages about kilohertz yield and refraction quotient of layers within my various sheets of combat armor, but a few give enough detail to be intriguing. Most of the weapon upgrades are geared towards fighting the increased resistance and resiliency of the Wraeththu mutants, while most of the armor upgrades are designed to filter out the kinds of electromagnetic interference that Tyse proved himself capable of producing. A lot of last minute adjustments made with our limited knowledge of the world beyond the Conduit in mind.

When I finally finish and make my way to the mess for a nutrition injection, I check the records and tracking for Lydecker, find a trail that indicates he's spent most of his time reviewing the findings in the local database that are at his moderate clearance level. During his stay, he's consumed three cups of synthetic coffee, two donuts and a bottle of water. Indulgences, and so many of them. Even his presence, his choosing to remain at Conduit Base, is an indulgence. He isn't needed on site, but then, he isn't really needed anywhere else either. Chief would recall him to The City if there was work for him to do. Perhaps it's easier to simply keep him on site in case something goes wrong and I need a ride back to Grey Division headquarters.

Curious, I check through the movement records of Hemmerly, Drake and Ibaraki. True to my expectations, Hemmerly's trail, his activities, everything about him is above my clearance level, totally inaccessible. The records on Doctor Drake and Doctor Ibaraki are less classified, however, and so I indulge myself for a few minutes, reviewing their activities. Ibaraki has spent most of the day interacting with Lydecker, logging in at terminals throughout the base to review summary reports from his subordinates, but Drake descended into The Pit hours ago and hasn't come back since. *'Final adjustments'* is the only notation I can find on his slated work for the day. Final adjustments, and an order for a pair of injectors of nutrient solution. Hard worker. Even takes his lunch on the go.

Sitting in the armory, indulging my curiosity out of an utter lack of anything else to do, I feel suddenly redundant, extraneous, useless, like an unneeded component waiting on a shelf. It's not a feeling I like, and so I close my eyes, call up a simple target-practice protocol on the back of my eyelids. It's comforting, meditative, hitting targets in my mind with a virtual lightrifle. It keeps me busy until the time comes for me to sleep, to rest my biological components and give my body time to repair and refresh itself.

I've heard that humans often have trouble sleeping the night before something important is scheduled to occur. There is a noticeable level of dissonance in my thoughts and nervous system, even with the meditative target practice, but I lock it down, as I always have in the past. As I lie down on the stiff cot I've been assigned for the next six and a half hours, protocols of augmented thought interact with the deeper coding of my mind, the mental machinery firing off responses in the glands and tissues that moderate my waking and sleeping states. In seconds, my eyes feel heavy, my shoulders sinking, hands hanging. In a breath, I'm gone, slipping away into serene darkness. Powering down.

Easy as flicking off a switch.

There is a sense of time passing in the night, but only the software, the lattice meshed into my neural tissue tracks it. For the rest of my mind, the meat side, the cultured and programmed animal side, there is only darkness, a blip of nothingness between waking states.

Coming back to consciousness, I run a quick cycle of mental diagnostics, find nothing out of the ordinary, nothing but the darkness, and that brings me a sense of peace. No dreams, no flickers of color or light. Such things are for humans, not for Valkyries, not for tools like me. Only those with souls ever dream, and that is fine with me.

A summary of updates ping through as my mind runs the coffee simulation, then taps into the local network. My three teams of Valkyries are scheduled to arrive in thirty-four minutes. Final checks are drawing to a close on the aperture device, and the Conduit is scheduled to be wedged open fifty-one minutes from now. Lydecker, Ibaraki and Drake are all in The Pit. I barely have time to rise, rub the sleep from my eyes and spin up a simple uniform simulation before Doctor Hemmerly walks through the door, regards me with his dark, wary eyes.

"How long have you been awake?" he asks.

I blink, clearing the last of the fog from my mind, wishing my biological neurons were as fast to fire up as the synthetic ones are. "Fifty-seven seconds."

"Cutting it kind of close, aren't you?"

"Close to what?" I study his features, the exhaustion at

the edges of his eyes, the broken blood vessels just beneath the surface of his cheeks that he tries to hide with modifications to simclothing software. Digital coverup, but with the enhancements to my eyes, I can see right through it all. He exhales heavily, and I pull in a trace of his breath, catch a faint alcohol reading.

"I told Lydecker I wanted you in The Pit during final checks this morning. Until the other Valkyries arrive, you're the only security we have on site, and I'd feel a lot better if you were watching the Conduit in case something comes through unexpectedly."

"I was not informed of that request."

"I noticed," he says, brow furrowing in irritation. "Now, if you're done with your beauty rest, could you please put on your field gear and get down to The Pit?"

"At once." I trigger the change, transition from uniform to combat armor so fast that it startles him. Taking even the smallest degree of pleasure in his reaction feels like an indulgence, but I enjoy it anyway. "If there's nothing else, sir…" I let the sentence trail off.

"Nothing else," he says, trying to keep the quaver out of his voice.

Machine-like, I fix my eyes ahead as I pass him, cross to the door and toward the hall beyond.

"Wait." It comes hesitant, quiet. When I half turn, regard him from the side with one eye, he swallows, hides his hands in his pockets. The change in demeanor, from anger to hesitancy makes my threat indicators flare up.

"There *is* something more," he says, and when he draws his hand from his pocket, augments in my vision catch a flash of steel, immediately identify the shape of a handgun, one of the matter weapons from the armory.

Every muscle in my body goes tense, but Hemmerly doesn't raise it, doesn't make any threatening gestures with it. Instead, he holds it by the front, hand on the slide, and presses the grip into my hand.

"Why are you giving me this?" I watch him carefully, eyes sharp, analyzing every movement of the muscles in his face. *Fear.* That's what I see. *Worry and fear.*

"Because we don't know what will happen when we widen the Conduit." His eyes rise to lock with mine. "We think we know. We've run the simulations, run projections and predictions for radiation profiles and electromagnetic flux, but they're all just that— simulations, projections, predictions."

"You have reason to believe that something will go wrong?" I turn to face him fully.

"Call it intuition." He looks away, gestures loosely, trying to act casual, dismissive. "A gut feeling."

Intuition. A human feeling. I blink, tune down my threat readiness with a breath, force myself back into a relaxed state. Hemmerly looks up again as I tuck the matter handgun away in a magnetic cache on my back, just at the beltline. I'm more apt to believe the simulations, projections and predictions of Hemmerly's team than I am to trust the gut feelings of a paranoid alcoholic, but I'm not about to turn down a weapon that could prove to be a tactical edge in the world waiting on the other side of the Conduit.

Because I know that in the field, every tactical edge has its place, its purpose.

"We should get to The Pit," I tell him, pulling him back, grounding him in the now again. In response, he only grunts, then nods and walks past me to the door. It actually surprises me a little when he waits for me at the threshold, clasps his hands behind his back and glances toward the central module of the base.

As a courtesy, I give him a soft smile, then follow, calling up an order for the delivery of an injectable breakfast as I go.

CHAPTER 8

There's a chill in the shaft over The Pit. A gentle gust, a feeling of movement downward, as if all the warm air from the portables is moving steadily into the darkness beneath us. As I step into the basic framework of the lift, I note the size of it, the rugged practicality. Enough room for ten people and equipment, and the whole thing is made from matter. Steel and aluminum, none of it light or EM.

Hemmerly's clothing flickers to something more bulky and utilitarian as he reaches for controls hardwired into the matter of the lift. Emitters in his skin spin up the thick lines and pads of a heavy hazard suit, open at the collar but sealed everywhere else. With a thought, he could probably call up a helmet as thick as the rest of the suit, and I wonder briefly how close that thought is, whether he holds a script for it ready in the grip of his forebrain, or leaves it loose, at the back of his mind.

The sudden, jerky movement of the lift pulls my attention back to the framework, checking for quivers in the matter, structural defects from overuse—anything that could be a danger to me or the doctor. Ideally, these things are checked regularly, but I have little experience with temporary matter elevators in the field, so it's easy to over-scrutinize the supports for stress marks and tension points in the metal. The wear and tear is average, I decide, having given cursory checks to every bolted joint and weld seam. A little wobble to the drop, but everything holds without protest.

"How far down is it," I ask Hemmerly, trying to

distract myself while coding kicks in to calm my physiology.

"A little over one hundred and fifty meters." He glances at me, turns as the lip of the portable above us gives way to a cross-section of glassy asphalt, pitted concrete and hard-packed clay dirt. The descent is steady, cuts right though the soil and granite toward some deep and unknowable darkness. "There's a network of caves and old mineshafts that honeycomb the whole area, providing several points of surface access to the Conduit, but navigating them takes hours, even if you know the way. Cutting a shaft right to the cavern where the Conduit was opened cuts that time to just a few minutes. Makes this whole project possible."

"Is there a shaft on the other side?" I glance at the walls around us, the passing glow of lights embedded in the granite, the channels cut through stone for long bundles of heavy insulated cabling.

"We don't know much about what's on the other side." Hemmerly crosses his arms, visibly uneasy again. "Interview feeds I've seen of Tyse seem to indicate that on his Earth, the Melorez Thorium Reactor incident never occurred. The area above us was rural and empty before the plague came and cleaned it out. The Dragon apparently built itself a home in the ruins and expanded downward, though how far or how comprehensively, I don't know."

"Far enough to protect itself from the Gelaming," I offer.

Hemmerly nods, says nothing. Not that there's time for it. A breath, maybe two, and then the shaft opens suddenly on a wide cavern filled with light and noise. Men and women in hazard suits like Hemmerly's hurry around a central bank of portable processing units, computer systems and databanks wired together with sprawling, segmented Conduits. The space itself is raw, all stone and dirt studded with lamps that bathe the place in soft, blue light. As the lift shivers to a stop, I spot John Lydecker in the midst of the rush, his long coat playing out an animation of a fashionable swish, as if there were enough of a gust at ground level to play with his clothing.

"Vaetta," he says as he crosses to the lift, smiling at me, practically ignoring Hemmerly. "The technology involved here is incredible. The calculations to widen the Conduit are so complex that they've got a dozen ARES processor packages banked into the aperture device—and they're overheating on every test, running right to capacity."

That's surprising, raises my eyebrows. From what I know of ARES processors, they're cutting edge, the latest in digital heavy lifting. A dozen of them banked together and they're still running hot? The amount of data they're crunching and extrapolating must be nearly unfathomable.

"Overheating?" Hemmerly asks, annoyed. "They shouldn't be." Even before he's off the lift and on the dirt floor of the cavern, he's shouting: "Drake! Dammit, Drake! You better not be toasting our processors!"

"You're early," Lydecker teases me. "But I guess, since you're with Doctor Hemmerly, he must have been the one who woke you and called you down here."

"He had security concerns." I give Lydecker the level response, try to ignore the subtle flush in his cheeks, the dilation of his pupils. I'm used to it from him, know what it means, know also that his attraction to me is fleeting and occasional. It's unusual for a human to be attracted to a labgrown subordinate, but with Lydecker, it isn't a threat. In the years I've known him, his attraction has never manifested as anything other than smiles and loose attempts at flirtation. For me, there is nothing there, nothing for him or anyone. Attraction, the sensation of it, feeling it—that is an indulgence for humans, for those with a soul.

"Security concerns, yeah." Lydecker looks away, and I follow his gaze, glance across the researchers, programmers and technicians preparing and cross-checking the aperture device with all of its connected systems. "We talked last night. Hemmerly's the only one who's worried, so I didn't take his request seriously."

"His intuition is troubling him." I step off the lift to stand beside John. The granite beneath my feet is solid and still, nothing like the endless, rhythmic hum of the roads and crowds of The City.

"As much as that man drinks, I think his intuition should be the least of his worries," John says, looking back to me. "We're coming up on thirty minutes 'til go. How do you feel?"

"Optimal," I answer simply.

"Optimal," John echoes. "No nervousness, eh? You're about to make history, Vaetta."

I fix him with a flat stare. "Humans get nervous, John. I have programming and integrated systems to lock down impulses like that."

"Right," he says, nodding, stuffing his hands in his simulated pockets. "Iron soldiers, a Valkyrie through and through."

"If I was anything less, Chief would have had me replaced."

"There is that." John nods, raising his eyebrows.

Another step puts me past him, puts me closer to the

bustle and lights of the heart of the project. My eyes rise and move from face to face, from console to console, passively scanning, finding exactly what I expect to—a handful of things that break the symmetry, a few false positives, a coffee mug sitting on the housing of one of the ARES processors, a handful of unencrypted security requests trailing in the wake of absent-minded researchers, but no genuine problems, no threats. John watches me silently as my eyes move from the people and the consoles to the machinery, the raw steel and shimmering lightworks of the aperture device, the thigh-thick cables and Conduits ready to pour power into the laser-precise hardware that will widen the tear in reality enough for me and my team to cross through.

"Can you see it?" Lydecker asks, gesturing.

"The Conduit?" I ask, and he nods.

Blinking, sending focusing and radiation-reading commands to the silicon in my augmented eyes, I stare at the spot where the rip should be, soak in all the faint readings I can. "There's nothing on the visible light spectrum. Some energy outside of that, but very little to read." I blink again, meet his eyes. "I can see where it is, but that's it."

"Wait until we open our link to the grid and pump enough power into it to dim an entire District," Ibaraki says, walking up, grinning at us. "I've seen this thing open up in some of our latest VR simulations, and if everything goes off without a hitch, I can say that it really will be a sight to behold."

Lydecker nods. "Looking forward to it."

"Your team is about twelve minutes out," Ibaraki says to me, tapping through a display projected against his wrist. He gestures to a space beyond the lift, at the opposite end of the cavern from the ARES processors. "You'll have this space to check them and brief them before you go."

"They will not need to be briefed," I tell him. "Any information on the operation they have not already received, they will be prompted to download when they arrive."

"Efficient." He nods, glances at Lydecker, then back to me. "It's my first time working with Valkyries."

"We'll be gone before you realize it." I offer him a soft smile, calculated to put him at ease, make him more effective in his capacity within the project.

"I envy you, seeing what's on the other side, *feeling it.*" Ibaraki smiles back. "I can't wait to go through the data when your team makes contact again."

"With sixteen of us running recording software, there will be plenty of it to go over."

"When are you scheduled to check in?" Lydecker asks.

"As soon as we're on the other side, and every hour, on the hour, if we can work with the Dragon to secure connections at regular intervals," I say. "Chief has set guidelines for contact with Conduit Base, and I plan to do what I can to meet them."

"There are a lot of variables that could delay contact," Ibaraki adds, provoking a curious glance from Lydecker. "Right now, we don't know how desperate things are for the Dragon. We don't know what energy reserves look like on the other side, and it takes an enormous amount of power to open the Conduit enough to even eke a data signal through."

"My team is equipped for assault operations," I offer. "We're prepared to handle any situation we might find when we arrive on Tyse's Earth. Even if the Gelaming mutants have breached the Dragon's defenses and are waiting for us to emerge from the Conduit, I'm confident we will be more than a match for them."

"Valkyries with lightrifles going up against modern Neanderthals?" Ibaraki whistles. "I know who I'd put my betting money on."

"That's if it comes to combat," Lydecker puts in, looking at me, as if hoping to see something besides the iron, the level stare. "There's still the hope for a diplomatic solution, last thing I heard. That's what Tyse was asking for. A peaceful resolution."

"If my team can lay the groundwork for colonization with a minimum of bloodshed, then a diplomatic solution may be possible."

"We'll have to wipe out the mutants eventually though, right?" Ibaraki asks, looking at both of us with hopeful eyes. "I mean, they're infected with a plague that's fatal at worst and disfiguring at best. We can push them into reservations and camps as a short-term solution but keeping them contained for any real length of time is just too risky. One escapee, and next thing you know, every colony could start reporting cases of infection."

Lydecker puts his hands in his pockets. "That's assuming we don't find a cure."

Ibaraki fixes his attention fully on the other man. "Their best scientists couldn't find a cure."

"As far as we know," Lydecker says. "But we're also more advanced, technologically, than this other Earth ever was, even at its peak." He pauses, offers a smile, but there's a sharpness to it, teeth. "Give our specialists a few weeks. I'm sure they'll find a cure."

I muse on Lydecker's optimism and Ibaraki's pragmatism. Both viewpoints have their merit, but in the end, it's my job to do the work, to navigate the minefields, both metaphorically and physically. When the lift near us rises, rattling up the shaft to collect what must be the first squad of my team, I pull in a deep breath, let it go.

Minutes. Mere minutes, and all speculation will be meaningless. Minutes, and I'll be in the thick of it. I'll be seeing Tyse's world first hand, immersed into all of its potential, as well as all of its harshness.

CHAPTER 9

Variation in Valkyries is subtle, mostly comes down to hair color, eye color, variations on cosmetic gene randomization that makes us all look a little different from one another. The biggest differences are from generation to generation, the places where the curves and lines of performance upgrades introduced in each new batch become visible.

Every one of the Valkyries Chief sends me is sixth-generation, the newest models. Looking over them, there's a slight softness, a curvature to the jaw, a minor decrease in height and in the width of the hips that sets us apart. As a fifth-generation model, I inspect them, study the tech notes on the adjustments to their synthetic and biological components, the justifications for each little change, but I feel no envy, no jealousy or sense of superiority. Functionally, we're identical. The differences count only for minor percentage increases on performance right out of the lab, count for little or nothing when compared to the adjustments we make ourselves as we mature.

No introductions, no briefings. Every member of my team recognizes me from the mission data the instant they step off the lift. One by one, they check in digitally, send their identification information and security codes directly to the silicon part of my brain. No nods, no handshakes, no words. Bonding is immediate, silent, an exchange of data that links us seamlessly, opens them to a private network where I can send quick commands at the speed of thought, direct them without wasting breath or time. On a surface level, I allow myself the indulgence of trait collation. *Seven shades of hair color, four of them variations on blonde. Five shades of eye color, three of them variations on brown. All earlobes attached. Recessive trait, not the dominant gene, not free-hanging like mine. That difference can't be cosmetic. Something the labs changed as a performance upgrade.*

A look at the tech notes confirms it. Justification: recessive trait: attached earlobes. Justification: soft tissues are minimally harder to tear off in combat.

Makes sense.

"Three minutes." Hemmerly's voice echoes through the cavern. There's a hum, an increase in ambient electromagnetic readings as components of the aperture device heat up, spin into readiness. "Grid is releasing holds on power. We're almost there. Watch those values, team."

The Valkyries sent by Chief gather around me in a knot as I turn to watch Hemmerly's team bring the aperture device online. Like a giant hand with a thousand steely, skeletal fingers, the machine seems to reach toward the focal point of all the radiation I've been reading. The Conduit—the breach between worlds. Power levels in the machinery climb, spike, and as they grow, those steely fingers start to glow, become white-hot, blurring into nothingness as if they were liquid, as if the steel itself were viscous, were being drawn steadily into the world beyond.

"Eighty percent." Hemmerly's voice comes over the speakers again, but the rumble, the keening of the device widening the rip between worlds obliterates most of what he says. The tension, the worry permeating every member of Hemmerly's team is palpable. Only we Valkyries stand even and unmoved, ready for whatever comes.

"We're crossing the threshold!" someone shouts, and then the klaxons start to howl, their sound distorted where it reverberates over and through the rippling wake of the Conduit. Even light and color seem to bend inward over the event horizon of the focal point, running in lines that curve harshly as the steel fingers flex. Like some kind of liquid membrane, the focus of all the energy pouring into Conduit Base begins to tear apart, rivulets of reality running across the aperture device, running back into the flux, the opening, the doorway between Tyse's world and ours.

And just when the howling, the wild light and the noise reach a crescendo, there's a command, a signal, and I pass it along to the Valkyries who follow me.

Forty-seven seconds. That's how long Hemmerly's team can keep the Conduit open wide enough for passage through. Forty-seven seconds.

Even single file, we make it through in twenty-eight.

There's no room for hesitation, no time to think twice, to do anything else but blindly sprint into that vortex of liquid color and twisting sound. Simple programs within my mind come alive, lock down every instinct to stop, to flee, to observe or reconsider. There isn't time. There isn't time for anything but a mad rush into the world beyond. Thought can come later. Thought can come when we're on the other side.

Even before I hit the Conduit, I can feel it. There's a moment, fifteen centimeters of indescribable tension and rush, of pull and push, of heat and ice washing across every inch of skin—and then I'm in it, slipping through the breach like rushing through a wall of water, like sprinting into a whirlpool that spreads out vertically instead of horizontally. There's an instant where my feet leave the ground, where I feel like I am flying, catapulted through void that is simultaneously scalding and freezing and nothing at all—and then I'm in the air again, in oxygen, dropping three feet toward a dirt floor in a cavern that, for an instant, looks almost identical to the one I just left.

But only for an instant.

The filaments of the web are so fine that I don't even register them until I hit them. Sticky strands slide across skin, cut through simulated armor like air and seal in against the flesh of my arms and legs, against every inch of me. Programs locking off the animal emotions within my mind crumble and fail—and then I'm screaming, thrashing against a net that is already sinking into my skin, blending with the meat and silicon of me. There's a voice inside my mind, a voice coming in from the filaments, a voice urging me to calm, to surrender, but there is also hunger in its sickly-sweet tone.

There is no hesitation in the way my team pours into the cavern and into the trap. Desperately, I tear at the filaments, try to free myself, but the bodies keep coming, keep falling, keep knocking me deeper into the stretching net. The walls of the cavern catch the terrified screeching, magnify it over the rushing noise of the Conduit, and then something beneath me gives way, tears loose and drops me into the dirt.

In less than a breath, I'm on my feet and sprinting, turning back toward the Conduit, hands already tearing the filaments out of my skin. My armor is shot, embedded emitters creating only flickers of wireframe plate, nothing solid. The web that spreads out beneath the whirling colors of the Conduit is huge, twisting and shaking as a dozen flickering Valkyries thrash against the filaments. There's hardly time for a thought, and then the last of my team falls into the web.

Time is short. Seconds, and the Conduit will close.

Experience, adrenaline, desperation—some part of me seizes my fear and catapults me toward the Conduit. It's six feet off the ground, but I clear the distance with a single jump, reach the event horizon just as it flashes around me, collapses away to a pinprick that feels cold and vacuous as it passes through my grasping fingers. When I hit the ground again, I feel the shock in my bones, in my wrists and thighs. Dirt in the air, dirt and screaming. I turn back to the web, and that's when I see them. That's when I realize that we're not alone.

They're small, silver, and they move fast, so fast. Spiders, or something like them, with long, bladed legs that catch light like glass. In swarms, they descend into the chaos, meld with the filaments of the web and burrow fluidly into flesh. I barely have time to throw commands into the failing emitters in my skin, to spin up an unreliable lightrifle before voices start to quiet, bodies going still. It takes every ounce of concentration I have to fight the static, the errors in the gun I've summoned, and even when I get a shot off, the tiny knot of lightning that lances from my lightrifle goes wide, dissipates into a crackle amidst the filaments of the shining web.

Quick breath, exhale and sigh of surrender. I let the lightrifle go, let it scatter into static. Hands clamber for the pistol at my back, the matter weapon Hemmerly gave me, but in the second and a half it takes me to draw it, to get it free, the spiders have already done their work. The last of my Valkyries goes silent, wrapped tight in a cocoon of silvered glass.

And the spiders keep coming. The swarms keep pouring from the ceiling, and now all of their little red eyes are fixed completely on me.

The matter weapon bucks against my hands, barks fire as I squeeze the trigger and smash one of the spiders into a cloud of powdered glass. Unphased, the swarms pour across the web, crawl over the bodies of my team and drop to the dirt to scurry toward me in a hungry, unstoppable wave. Immediately, it becomes clear that I don't have enough bullets to free my people. With one clip in the matter gun, I doubt I even have enough bullets to protect myself. In the moment, I remember that the lift wasn't the only way to the surface in my own Earth's analog of the cave, that there were other ways, miles of caverns and mineshafts honeycombing through the granite of the Gold Country.

Spinning away, matter handgun gripped tight in the flickering glove of my light-based assault armor, I do the only thing I can think to do. Muscles flex, thighs coming alive, and then I'm sprinting again, sprinting hard for the first opening in the cavern that I can see. It's small, dark, looks ragged and natural, not cut by man. I rush through even as the static in my augmented vision fails to pick out details, sends me careening off crumbling stone at a sudden bend in the passage, and I'm hoping it isn't just a fissure, won't just dead end and trap me for the spiders. When it widens, opens to light again, I almost breathe a sigh of relief. Almost, but the sudden presence of a dozen humanoid shapes cut in black glass and chrome keeps me from stopping for even an instant.

The first round that flies punches through my thigh with expert accuracy—a shot intended to stop me, immobilize me. There's a shriek, a sound that tears through my teeth as I hurl myself down another passage, fight against the searing pain in my leg. Failing programs bridging the meat and silicon of my mind fight to lock down the pain, to keep me moving, but every spike of static and heat that cuts through the haze costs me speed, makes me stumble. Other shots lance into the stone around me, narrowly missing as I duck and weave, using every scrap of cover I can find to keep from taking any more bullets. In the passageway behind me, I hear the spiders and the soldiers, the humanoids of black glass and chrome. I hear them all, the rhythm of them, the sounds of machines pounding the dirt of the cavern floor in relentless pursuit.

And then I round a corner and find myself face-to-face with one of them. An arm, all pistoning silver and taut wires reaches for my shoulder, clamps an inch from flesh as I throw myself forward, press the matter weapon hard against black glass and put two rounds square in the face of the thing. Stunned and flailing, sharp fingers snap at me as I shove it over, knock it into dirt and leave it without even looking back. Two more of the drones come at me, matter weapons rising, taking aim, but I pivot to the side, tackling one and knocking it into the other. In the time it takes them to untangle themselves, I'm already gone, darting down another darkened tunnel, desperate for breath, for light.

At some point, the machines stop coming. At some point, I lose them in the twisting, dusty passages. The wound in my leg weeps slow but steadily, grinds down my strength and adrenaline until it's all I can do to lope through tunnels, hoping for a way out. Every synthetic system in my body is flickering, unreliable—even the nanomechanical coagulants that should have sealed the bullet hole hours ago are having trouble working together, losing cohesion almost as often as they achieve it.

I don't know how many hours pass before I finally stop. Static in my mind gives an unreliable reading of time elapsed, but it feels like hours, two or three at least. With no way to tell how deep I am within the caves and no map charting where I might find a way out, I start to question the wisdom of running endlessly, finally settle down against the rocks in the darkness to catch my breath.

Protocol kicks into gear almost immediately. A quick diagnostic of my synthetic systems shows corruption, interference. Parsing through inconsistent data, it seems that the problem is as much some lingering effect of contact with the web as it is simply something in the environment around me. The data I can pull from accumulated profiles of intermittent ambient electromagnetic interference hints at something huge, an incredible amount of activity several hundred meters above me, but no indication as to what it is.

Corruption in my systems I could handle with a visit to a Grey Division clinic. Given enough time and data, shielding upgrades could be designed to overcome the ambient interference. Cut off as I am from my own world, my own people, neither of those is an option, so I focus inward, try to calm myself, do what I can to stabilize my synthetic systems. None of it works. I give up after fifteen minutes or so of staring at my flashing, flickering hands in the dark, trying to get my projected armor to solidify.

There is a moment where I allow myself to be afraid. It's brief, an indulgence. Without my team, my equipment, my emitters, and without access to the Conduit, my options for survival, for accomplishing the goals of the mission are extremely limited. With the Dragon now clearly classifiable as a threat, I'm stranded deep in enemy territory with no clear allies and no clear means of escape. All I have left is my memory, my wits, and a matter weapon with seven rounds left in the clip.

And time is running out. I'm bleeding, and it doesn't look like it's going to stop.

CHAPTER 10

Tracing my way back toward the Conduit seems like the only viable option. Working through the tunnels, I do my best to cover my tracks, cover the drops of blood that fall from the wound in my leg. In my mind, I make a mental map, track every branching corridor and listen at every juncture for the sounds of pursuing machines. Whenever I find a cavern or tunnel that slopes toward the surface, I take it, study it. Sometimes, I'm forced to backtrack.

The tunnels themselves are raw, barren and dark. Granite, primarily, with some limestone, most naturally carved, some with marks that show they were cut with iron tools long ago. Here and there, I find evidence of old mineshafts, walls and ceilings braced with stout beams of rotten wood. Not once do I find anything to cover myself with, to bind my wound with. Not a scrap of cloth. Nothing.

The flickers in my armor make enough light to see by, barely, but in the end I give up and kill the projections utterly, feeling my way through the darkness, judging direction and dangers by the sensations of air against my naked skin. Here and there, I find the glow of artificial light, but always I shy away from it. Only once do I brave it, darting through a wide cavern lit by flashing running lights to another darkened tunnel beyond. For minutes afterward, I pick my way along slowly, tensely, listening for sounds of pursuit. Thankfully, none come.

When I finally reach the steps of a staircase hewn into the stone, part of me starts to relax. It's the most human thing I've seen so far, and it gives me some hope that I might be near the surface. When it dead-ends at an iron gate chained with a stout lock that has to be over a hundred years old, the hope I've felt suddenly seems hollow and fleeting.

Briefly, I consider turning around. The tunnel beyond the gate is dark, could lead anywhere, but hunger, fatigue and frustration get the better of me. Slowly, I raise the matter weapon, point the barrel at the lock and pause. The metal is rusty in places. There are weak points where a round might be able to breach and disable the mechanism, but shrapnel and noise are considerations. Firing a gun in the caverns seems like the surest way to bring every one of the Dragon's machines down on me in an instant, and if the passageway beyond is a dead end, then all the running I've done will be for nothing.

I'm the last of my team, with no clear way home. Locking down my fear, I press the matter weapon against the lock, pull the trigger.

The hot bite of iron shrapnel ripping across skin hits me before the bark of the gun and the squeal of metal does. The harsh smell of cordite and ozone burns my nose. Desperate, I tear at the lock with my bare and bleeding hands, yank at it, but it doesn't give. The iron is too strong. The mechanism still holds.

Again, I pull the trigger, and again I feel the heat and bite as splinters from the lock pelt my face, my hands. Shrieking, shouting, I try to pull the lock apart, end up rattling the chain against the gate, making even more noise. On the third shot, the lock finally splinters and gives, but I have to hurl myself against the gate to get the rust to break away from the hinges. When the metal starts to move, it shifts slowly, heavily, and the noise it makes is deafening.

Ten seconds, maybe twenty. That's all I get, and then there is movement at the base of the staircase. Rounds zip quick through the darkness, hit bars, ring through the gate mere centimeters from my neck and face. Every bit of my skin feels warm, burning, and there's blood on my hands, slick against the grip of the firearm. It's everything I can do to rush up the staircase, to take it five steps at a time until I reach another gate, another lock and chain wrapped around iron bars.

And beyond, seven concrete steps beyond, I can see sunlight.

Steel rings against steel. I know the humanoid machines are close. I know that if I can't get through this last gate, I'm dead. They'll catch me, do to me what they did to my team, and that's if I'm lucky. The first shots were low, aimed to disable. The last two rounds were aimed with killing intent.

My hands are slippery with running blood. I pull the lock loose, position it against the bars of the gate, then blast it until it falls off. With the last shot, the slide on the gun draws back, the breech open and empty. Tearing open the gate, I glance back, catch the glint of light off black glass, a dozen faceplates moving in the darkness— then turn and sprint as hard as I can for the sun. Rounds zip into concrete, narrowly missing me, throwing dust into the air, and then I'm on the streets of a gutted city, out in the open, with trees and brush and nature crowding in from every direction.

Overwhelmed, I hesitate, but the squeal of metal bodies pushing on the gate gets me moving again. The sun is low in the sky.

My knowledge of Old Cali is scant and probably totally worthless on this alien Earth. I know that the sea and the cities are probably to the west, the colder climes to the east. One glance picks out a highway, channels where rivers cut through stone. Rough terrain, easy to get lost in. Ten meters to a broken bridge over the rocks of a seasonal creek, and I'm out of sight again, gone before the drones can even reach the surface.

The clay soil along the bank of the dry creek is rough and rocky beneath my bare feet, chunks of ragged basalt biting while smooth river rocks press into my arches. The creek runs for several hundred meters before I find a break in a chainlink fence on the other side, dive across and through into a sprawling lot of dead grass. Golden, waist-high and full of burrs that catch my hair, scratch my thighs and ankles as I run, the grass is even easier to get lost in. It hurts like hell, running, bleeding, but I force myself to put almost half a kilometer between me and the drones before I dare to stop, inspect my wounds, consider my options.

The grass pours down the steady slope of a treeless hill, descends into a gully that runs like a narrow seam of green between two golden rises. At the bottom, I turn, follow the trickle of water south until I find trees, a little copse where gnarled roots bend into the cool, pooling stream.

In the shadows, I check my wounds. Superficial, mostly, with the exception of the one in my leg. Slivers of iron, from the locks I shot through, stand out here and there on my skin, but come free with a little digging and pulling. Blood loss has compromised my performance, made me weak and pale, so I make binding my wound the next priority. With no bandages, no way to seal or suture my thigh, I'll have to get creative.

I spend a few minutes testing the tensile strength of the

grass, find it lacking. The trees have hard, thin bark that might be useful as tinder, but not much else. Even the leaves are small and dry, alive, but evolved to conserve water. Nothing I can use on my wound.

It feels like a desperate, last-ditch measure when I remember the matter weapon I'm carrying. Steel, capable of taking enough heat to cauterize wounds. Thinking about it is enough to make me hesitate, hoping that some other option will come to mind, but nothing does. There is only one way, I decide. One course, and if I want to survive, I have to take it.

Building a fire is out of the question. The smoke would make me visible, draw anyone in the area right to me before I could recover enough to run again. Only one source of heat I can think of, and it will take patience, focus.

Somewhere in the database of tactical knowledge installed within the silicon side of my mind, I manage to find instructions that give me all I need to break down the matter weapon and pull the steel recoil pin from the assembly. Careful not to lose the recoil spring, I set all the parts aside where I can see them, hold the finger-thick pin in front of my eyes, inspect it, ready myself for what I'm about to do. Confidence comes with a deep breath, a steady exhale, and then I set the pin in the center of my left palm, focus on the emitters there.

At first, nothing happens. A quick diagnostic kicks back results, readings on the staggering amount of ambient interference permeating everything on the surface. The lingering corruption from the web is still present, but even its effect is minimal compared to whatever is bombarding the whole area with enough electromagnetic energy to kill the emitters in my skin completely.

Frustrated, I stare at my palm, swap the recoil pin and try to focus on the emitters in my other hand. Minutes pass, minutes where I slip into a place of intensity and turn my entire focus inward, trying to summon up the barest glow of heat, but nothing comes. Diagnostic after diagnostic returns the same results. Interference, and too much of it to overcome.

In the end, I'm tempted to throw the pin as hard as I can in a moment of indulgent rage. It feels important, like it would satisfy something in me, but rationally I know that it would only make things more hopeless than they already are. Instead, I hold the pin up between my index finger and thumb again, stare at it indignantly, as if maybe it could somehow feel my rage, as if it were capable of understanding and changing.

Eventually, I put the recoil pin back in the matter weapon, piece the whole thing back together and set it beside my weeping thigh. The blood loss is minimal, but doesn't show any signs of stopping. Cauterization or stitches—not much else is going to keep me from bleeding out during the night, and I don't have access to either. Clothing, weaponry—everything I've carried with me, with the exception of the empty matter weapon, is light-based, powered by the emitters in my skin. With the interference, I'm stripped of everything I need to survive. With the interference, I'm naked, utterly defenseless and bleeding to death in the middle of nowhere on an alien Earth.

And now, the sun is going down.

CHAPTER 11

With darkness comes the hunger and the cold. I try to fill my belly with water in the final minutes of light after the sun slips below the horizon, try to find something to eat that won't poison me. Nibbling on leaves and running tests on dietary values turns up red flags everywhere. Nothing in the copse has any nutritional weight to it, and most of it is bitter with toxic levels of tannic acid. Better just to try to stave off the hunger until the morning, if I live that long. At least the water in the stream is mostly clean.

Fighting with the programming in the silicon side of my mind, I do the best that I can to forge an ad hoc field patch to repair my ability to resist pain and cold. Locking down the impulse to shiver is the hardest part, but by the time the temperature falls through twelve degrees Celsius, I've got it handled. Focus comes back, a little at a time, and then I'm watching the darkness, searching for lights, however faint, and listening to the little noises of nature and the night.

Until I realize that I'm not alone.

It happens suddenly, a pinprick of awareness exploding into clarity. There's breath, a palpable warmth in the air just off to my right, maybe seven meters at most. There's a sensation that something huge is close, blocking out the darkness in the way that only a body can. Not machine, I realize. There's a scent to it, organic, subtle.

The scent of an animal. An apex predator.

Terror. A sense of shared knowing. The stall of regular breath, the sudden release of an animal scent of fear. The predator moves even before I do, leaps at me, brushing skin as I catapult myself straight up into the overarching branches of a tree, scramble toward the highest point of night I can find. The tree is squat, branches steady enough to climb for only maybe the first twelve meters, and then it turns into springy, dry foliage. On the bank below, I hear the scattering of stones, the shift of movement, and then nothing. *Nothing.*

Adrenaline surges inconsistently through my body. I hate the weakness I'm feeling, the physical functionality that has been stripped away steadily since I stepped through the Conduit. Whatever is on the ground, I should be able to fight it, subdue it, even eat it, maybe. I shouldn't be running. I shouldn't be hiding, clinging to branches in a desperate attempt to stay alive.

I don't know how long I stay in the tree. Sitting motionless, I listen, follow the noises of the night, but whatever lunged at me has gone utterly silent. Insects start to chitter and sing again in sporadic knots, and still I wait in the tree, wait for something that never comes.

At some point, I hear the cry of a night bird, distant at first, then closer and closer until it settles on a branch less than a meter from me. The little thing is so noisy, so confident, but the instant it catches the sound of my breathing and the scent of my skin, it freezes, goes utterly silent for a breath, then flees, calling out as it goes. I wait until the cries fade into the distance, until all the sounds of the gully return full force, and still there is nothing, no sign of the apex predator.

Only when I finally lower myself from the branches to the stones of the shore do I realize that the predator never left. Only then do I realize how quiet, how patient the beast has been.

The impact comes before I can react. Huge, dark—the shape rises and hits me right in the guts, grabs me and slams me against the trunk of the very tree I'd been hiding in. There's heat, pressure, but no bite, nothing but a clamping tightness. Terrified, I shriek and tear at the shape, find my hands suddenly seized in a fist, light exploding into my eyes.

"Name!" The creature barks, and the voice is harsh, cut with fury, even hate.

"Gelaming!" I scream the first word that comes to my mind. "Let me go!"

"Liar!" The shape snarls back. "I know a Gelaming when I see one! You're not even har!" The light dips suddenly down the length of my body, rises again. "You're... you're *female!* What the hell!?"

"Let me go!" I demand again, but the grip just gets tighter.

"I saw you leave the caves!" he spits back. "I saw the drones come to the surface, then turn back." His fist bites into my skin with a harshness that is almost blinding. "What the hell is going on!?"

"Can't... breathe." I fake it, give his arm a weak squeeze. When he takes the bait, backs off his grip a little, I tear free of his fists, throw myself at him and carry him to the ground. The light goes spinning away down the shore, throwing crazy shadows over everything. Fists come at me again, but this time, I'm quicker. One solid punch to the jaw is enough to stun him, and then I'm on my feet again, scrambling down the rocky slope after the flashlight. Behind me, I hear the figure rising, the scrape of boots on stone, the grunt and snarl of rage. I reach the flashlight an instant before he reaches me, and as I spin, I bash one of his grabbing hands with the club end, hard enough to make the bulb flicker.

The roar of pain is deafening, buys me time. Rushing along the shore, I find the place where I left the handgun, scoop it up and point it directly at the figure as he rises. The muzzle is clear and chrome as I hold it out to the side of the light, a direct threat to anyone who doesn't know the clip is empty. Instead of putting up his hands, the figure only turns to me, looks at me with tired eyes, with blood running from his angry lips.

And that's when realization hits me.

"Tyse?" The name explodes from my lips.

A matching look of confusion flickers across Tyse's face as he stares back at me, blinks against the harshness of the light. I can't say how, but it is him, unmistakably so.

"How do you know my name?" he asks, hunching a little, favoring the hand I bashed with the flashlight.

"What are you doing here?" I demand. "How did you get back?" Then, as fear sets in, I spit out: "I won't end up like the others. I'll shoot you before I'll end up like the others."

"What the fuck are you talking about!?" he snarls back. "What kind of bullshit game is this!?"

"Answer me!" I scream.

"You first!" he screams back.

I swallow, pull back a little, trying to reign in my emotions. An impasse, and neither one of us is going to break it while we're too locked in adrenaline to do more than shout at each other.

"Are you a clone?" I ask him, softer than previously. "How many are there in your series?"

"A clone?" He shakes his head. "No, I'm not a clone."

He could be lying, but it feels like progress. His eyes

follow mine, sharp and unwavering.

"Now answer one of my questions," he demands. "Why were you in the caves?"

You know why I was in the caves. I want to spit it at him, scream the words in his face, but I lock the emotions down, force calmer words. "It's a long story."

"I'm not going anywhere."

"Your leader..." I swallow, try gathering words. "The leader of your tribe asked us to come."

Tyse shakes his head. "I don't have a tribe. I haven't had one for years."

"You asked us to come!" I shout back at him. "You told us your tribe was under attack by the Gelaming! You begged us!"

"I've never met you before today!" he barks at me, then shakes his head, scoffs. "Why are you here? Why are you...?" He makes a frustrated gesture. "Why are you *naked*!?"

I pull in a deep breath, try to steady myself. "The webs. The webs, and the interference out here." I pause, give him a level stare. "That's why I'm naked. My emitters— they can't work past it."

"The *webs* and the *interference out here?*" He looks at me incredulously. "You sound crazy, you know that? You sound totally fucking batshit crazy." He gestures again. "I mean, yeah, you look like you fit the very model definition of *nuts* in so many ways right now, but..." He pauses. "How do you know my name? You were programmed to know it, weren't you? You're some kind of experiment gone wrong, something the Dragon created..."

"My name is Vaetta." I cut him off, let the words spill out as fast as I can. "Currently engaged in an operation for Grey Division. My commission number is V1041 Kappa. You and I—we met while you were incarcerated in the holding area of Level Delta at Headquarters..."

"I..." Tyse shakes his head, cutting me off, but I forge ahead anyway.

"I'm not finished!" I shriek. "We met in the holding area of Level Delta. We talked about this Earth, *your Earth!* I have hours of feed footage stored in digital I can replay at any time, footage of you telling myself and others about this Earth, about the Gelaming threat to the Dragon. You pleaded with us to help you, to save the Dragon. You gave us the technology needed to cross from one Earth to another. We used your Conduit to come here, and that is when your tribe betrayed us. The trap— my entire team was lost in the trap. I barely escaped with my life. I'm not going back. I'll kill you before I let you take me back."

Tyse swallows, straightens his back a little. There's something in his features I can't read, a paleness, a worry. When he talks again, his voice is calm, quiet.

"Okay," he says. "Okay, obviously there's a lot more going on here than makes sense to me right now." He pauses, shakes his head, considering. "I don't know who you talked to, but it wasn't me. I'm no friend of the Dragon. I tolerate the Gelaming. Hell, I even trade with them once in a while, share coffee with—but that's not the point." He squints, chooses his words carefully. "You say you crossed from one *Earth* to another. You—what *other* Earth?"

I mull his words over in the silence, considering my response. There's an innocence to his tone that makes it easier to trust him, but I'm not completely convinced he's not just trying to confuse me, so he can drag me back to the caves.

"The Earth I left is different. The Dragon reached out to us. It created the Conduit between our Earths and sent you—sent someone calling himself Tyse, someone who looks like you. That Tyse gave us the technology to cross back here." I pause a moment, breathe a shaky sigh. "On my Earth, things have happened differently. The City stretches across almost the entire planetary surface. There aren't wide, natural areas like this—this place." I gesture at the trees, the sprawling land around us. "Humans and labgrown people make up the entire population. On my Earth, the plague never happened. Wraeththu never came to be."

There's a moment while Tyse looks away, a moment while he seems stunned, unable to process the words. When he drops back to a sitting position, I lower the gun a little, but not entirely.

"This is..." He pauses, gesturing. "This is *a lot*. I'm not really sure I understand everything." He looks up at me again, staring, and then something changes. The last of his anger starts to fade, and something else rises in its place. *Concern? Empathy?* "Aren't you cold? Put that gun away. Stop waving it around like you're going to shoot someone. Damn thing isn't even loaded."

I hesitate, keeping the matter weapon on him for a moment more. When I finally decide there's no use in continuing the ruse, I drop into a crouch, set the gun on the stones at my feet.

"Here." He takes off his coat, holds it out to me. It's fabric, real fabric, and shows the grime that only comes with long-term use. In my hands, it feels heavy, warm. I almost turn it down, would turn it down if I wasn't so cold, if I had any other choice.

Tyse smiles when I take the coat, wrap myself up in it.

"I'm going to start a fire," he says, rubbing his hands together briskly.

"Won't they see?" I ask, watching him worriedly.

"The drones?" He makes a dismissive gesture. "Yeah, but I got a trick to fix that. Nothing a little magic won't take care of."

"Magic?"

"Or something like it." He nods, standing up to gather sticks and sheaves of dry grass. "Whatever you want to call it. I've learned how to blend in here, hide my heat, and the heat and light of the fires I make. Only way to stay alive this close to the caves."

"I think..." I hesitate. "I have a lot of questions."

"You and me both," he says, gesturing again. "Here, help me get all this together. Once we get some heat, maybe we can figure out some answers. While I cook us dinner, you can tell me about your Earth, how you got your wounds, and how you got here."

Dinner. I can't help licking my lips. Finally, there's hope. A shred but hope nonetheless.

Chapter 12

Night moves fast, keeps my eyes wide with wonders. Even without the use of emitters, Tyse manages to start a fire with a point of light gathered in the palms of his hands. I can't explain it, and he laughs as I take his hands in mine and try to figure out where the heat has come from.

"How does it work?" I ask him, but all he can say is that it does. It comes from focus. He sees the fire, sees the heat already rising, and suddenly it *simply is*.

Following his example, I try to summon my own fire, but nothing comes.

"Keep trying," Tyse tells me. Then he stands and spreads his arms to the sky. He begins to bend the light subtly, as if he were capable of reaching to the very stars themselves, dimming them in waves just for an instant, just enough to hide the heat and smoke of our fire. Awestruck, I forget entirely about trying to summon my own fire, watch the strange ripples in reality as they spread out from his fingers instead.

"What else can you do?" I ask.

"Quite a bit." He grins, then gestures. "I've seen you favoring your leg, and I've seen the blood. How badly hurt are you?"

Pulling in a deep breath, I pull up the hem of the coat enough to show him the hole in my thigh. It's clean, small caliber. Matter weapon, but probably the work of a steel plug driven by a magnetic coilgun.

"Yep, looks like they shot you." Tyse reaches for the wound, and it takes every bit of resolve I have not to flinch at his touch. "Drones, definitely. Deep too."

"It won't stop bleeding." I focus on keeping still, try not to think about how dirty his hands are as he touches the skin around the wound. "With my synthetic systems malfunctioning, it will need to be cauterized, or sutured."

"I've got something better." He gives me a wry grin, holds up a hand. "Watch this."

Again, I have to resist the urge to flinch and pull away.

Hands hover over the wound, and then suddenly there's heat, a subtle glow rippling in the space between my skin and the palm of his hand. It's mesmerizing, the way it reaches deep into the muscle, soothes away the pain instead of burning, instead of scalding. I know my mouth is hanging open by the time the wound is sealed, and seeing my awe only makes Tyse grin wider.

When he settles back beside the fire, I can tell he's exhausted, even more so than before. Amazed, I run my hands over the place where the wound was, find only the subtle line of a scar instead. Standing suddenly, I test the muscle, check for pain, run simple diagnostics on performance response. *Optimal.* It's incredible. Tyse's work is cleaner, quicker and more effective than anything I've experienced at any of the Grey Division clinics back on my own Earth. It's almost as if I'd never been shot at all.

"You're obviously not from around here," he says, watching me. "You even *feel* different than anyone I've ever met. You don't feel like something the Dragon made, that much is clear to me now. Everything he touches seems to have his stink in it, his hate." He pauses, gets to his feet slowly. "I can sense the metal in you, yeah, but it feels different than anything I've felt of the Dragon's technology." I watch as he crosses to his backpack, starts to rummage in it, comes up with a couple of rusty cans labeled only with the scrawl of a permanent marker. "You must come from a very interesting world."

"Interesting?" I turn to him, watch as he slides a blade into one of the cans, separates the lid from the cylinder with smooth ease. "Different, certainly."

"I want to hear about the differences," he says. "Tell me what the people are like where you come from."

Where to begin? Between pre-programmed knowledge and personal experience, I could talk for hours about my Earth. I could give a dozen lectures and bore him out of his mind with studies and meaningless historical details. I could rattle off the specifications of common cybernetic skin lacings or talk about tactics until the sun comes up. Judging from what I know of Tyse, what I know from my time with both versions of him, and what I know of humans, I try to stick to the basics, the details relevant to my past, the course that brought me here.

For hours, I talk with Tyse about The City, about the people who live within it, about Chief, Lydecker, the divisions in society between rich and poor, between labgrown tools like myself and genuine humans. Mostly, he listens in silence, absorbing, only breaks my rhythm to ask questions, to ask me to explain terms he's never heard before. Choosing my words carefully, I make the whole operation that has stranded me in his Gold Country sound like a purely humanitarian mission, omit everything concerning colonization and more of my people coming through the Conduit. At some point, he offers me a bowl of something warm and musky, which he calls *beef stew*. I'm so hungry that it's easy to ignore the smell, the bizarre textures and taste sensations that come with orally consuming hot, canned food. Even between bites, I keep the narrative going, tell him about my interactions with the other Tyse, the technology involved in bridging alternate Earths together through the use of the Conduit. When I start talking about crossing into the caves from my own Earth, he offers me a crumpled, hand-rolled cigarette stuffed with some rank-smelling weed, but I turn it down politely. The smoke is dizzying, laced with sedatives, hypnotics—I find myself leaning out of it as he puffs, and eventually he gets the message, waves the stink away with his hands even as he continues to listen.

"We have to tell the Gelaming," he says, and it comes in the moment of silence that follows the story of my escape from the caves. "Tomorrow morning." He stubs out the cigarette. "This is important."

"Can they be trusted?" I ask him.

"No." He stands, a little shaky on his feet. "But they're the ones who do most of the work to keep the Dragon in check on the surface. I've been trying to get them to come into Cinder Hill, into the caves and destroy it for years, but they never listen. They'd rather contain it, study it." He makes a dismissive gesture. "I've fought this thing before. Hell, I've been fighting the machine mind in these hills for most of my life as a har. This..." He points at me. "You, and your story, the Conduit, all of it." He makes a fist, holds it. "This might be enough for us to finally get them to take aggressive action. Your story proves that containment has failed. The Dragon is spreading, it just isn't spreading where they can see it."

Briefly I think of Chief, of my mission. Pitting the Gelaming against the Dragon, letting them tear each other apart, making room for my people, the colonial forces from my Earth. It almost sounds too good to be true.

Adrenaline spikes within me, just briefly, and I swallow in response, locking it down. Can't get ahead of myself. Meeting the Gelaming, assessing the strength of their forces comes first. *Tomorrow.*

"I think..." I nod. "Tomorrow morning. Yes."

"They're gonna love you." He grins. "A half-human, half-machine soldier from another world? Too bad you're a woman. If your people had sent men, the Gelaming would probably try to incept you before even shaking your hand."

"Incept?" I ask.

"Make you into one of us." He chuckles. "One of us—what did you call us? *Plague mutants?*"

"Because of the disease," I put in quickly, trying to deflect from any offense I might have caused.

"I prefer to think of it as a blessing." Tyse's smile softens. "A lot's happened to me since I became har. A lot of bad things, but learning myself, learning how to manifest abilities like what I've shown you tonight—I'm happier. I'm growing, growing and maturing in ways I never could have dreamed of. We all are. Whatever it is that makes us Wraeththu, whatever it is that's in the blood—I'm glad I was incepted. Most hara I know are happier now than they ever were as humans."

Mutants still, I tell myself. *Happy or not, you're no longer human. You're infected, and that makes you an active danger to humankind.*

"We should sleep," he says suddenly, reaching for his pack again. "I have two blankets, but I can tell from the chill in the air that there's going to be frost in the morning." He pauses a moment, as if considering his words. "If you're open to it, we could share, conserve body heat."

Logically, it makes sense. Indulging my fear of vulnerability, of what he might do, what he might try to do during the night, seems almost foolish given how cold it already is. So far, he's given no indication that I cannot trust him, no *clear* indication. After a moment of internal debate, I finally side with caution and shake my head.

"No," I say. "You keep the blankets. I can go for days without sleep." I settle a little deeper into the coat, creep closer to the fire. "I'll keep the fire and watch for drones. You sleep."

"Suit yourself," he says, and it comes soft, casual, without malice.

As he beds down for the night, I watch him settle in, note the way he keeps his knife on him, drawn and at his side, hand resting lightly on the hilt. The gesture isn't overt, but I have a feeling that if he had wanted to hide the knife, he could have.

A warning. That's how I choose to take it. That's all I hope it is.

The fear, the worry that it might be something else more ominous is what keeps me fighting to stay awake all night long.

CHAPTER 13

I don't know if Tyse sleeps, or if he only pretends to. Five times during the night, the synthetic side of my brain fails me, and I find myself waking up, gone for a few minutes at most, sleeping and vulnerable nonetheless. Panic grips me with every return to consciousness, but always I find Tyse still in his bundle of heavy, ragged blankets, facing away from the fire, moving only with the slight rhythm of steady breathing. A moment of focus brings me back to a place of steadiness, and then, invariably, I realize that the fire has gone low, my bladder is full, or both.

Gathering more dry grass, breaking down sticks and chunks of dead wood gets me out of the copse here and there, gets me out under the stars, beneath a sky unlike anything I've ever seen on my Earth. With clear air, a total lack of lights and pollution, the heavens shine above me like a great and glittering dome, and even as cold as the night gets, I can't help but stare. There's something about it, something about the brilliance of the stars, the way the widest band of them stretches up from the horizon in the south like the trunk of a great tree, towering over everything. There's something, and it pulls at me, even though I cannot put a name to it, to the feeling within me.

An indulgence, I decide, but stranded as I am, and cut off from my own Earth, I can allow myself some minor indulgences. Lingering under the stars, admiring an alien sky feels harmless enough.

The last time I jolt awake, there's a subtle light to everything, a crisp, gray glow washing away all the glittering points embedded in the heavens. Dawn, and slow-coming. I gather one last armload of sticks and grass, stoke the fire and huddle up next to it, waiting for Tyse to wake up.

It isn't long before he's moving, rolling over and blinking blearily at the coals, at me, as if trying to remember who I am, why I'm there. "Did you get any sleep?" he finally asks me.

"No," I lie. "I stayed up watching the stars."

"I guess there are worse ways to spend a night," Tyse says, stretching. "Why the fascination? They don't have stars on your Earth?"

"They do, but they aren't as bright," I tell him. *And they don't call to me like the stars here do.* That much I leave unspoken. It's probably just an error in processing, a sensation thrown off by corruption, fragmentation of data. "The skies are very clear here."

He nods. "Been a long time since human industry was in full swing. Cars are rare these days. I think about the only pollution you'll find anymore is smoke from campfires, and with the drones out here, even those are sparse outside of Irulin."

"Irulin?" I ask, absently poking the fire with a stick, watching the sparks dance.

"Where we'll find the Gelaming," Tyse says, sitting up, dragging himself into wakefulness. "It's a tent town, real small, about ten miles northeast of Cinder Hill, up old Highway 88." He pauses a moment, thoughtful. "I used to live there. Busier now since the Gelaming came in and took over."

"Took over?" I ask.

"Long story," Tyse says, waves it away dismissively. "Short version is, I had a tribe once. We lived in Irulin, but we called it by its old Human Era name—Segerstrom

Ranch. When the Dragon slaughtered everyhar I ever cared about, I couldn't bring myself to go back. I stayed in the hills here, did what I could to harass the Dragon. At some point the Gelaming claimed the land and renamed it." He shrugs, lets the sentence hang.

"You really are all alone out here, aren't you?"

When Tyse looks at me, his eyes are sharp, distant. He looks lost in thought, but also wary, watching me as if trying to see beneath the words, see through them to some hidden core. When he finally responds, it's a nod, quick and simple, and then he's in his backpack again, digging for something.

"How many years has it been, Tyse?" I ask, picking at the knots in my hair.

"Too many," is the only response I get. Gruff and quick, but not mean, not angry. When he rises again, he tosses me something leathery, something thick, like a strip of soft, brown rubber. "Breakfast," he says, gesturing, then turns back to his pack, taking a bite out of his own strip of leathery food. Curious, I turn the thing over in my hands, studying it, trying to discern what it is. Bits of ground-up something stick out from the surface, some kind of dried plant material, or seeds...

Tyse stops, sees me studying the strip, watches as I wipe the grease from it on the lining of his coat.

"Jerky," he says to me, as if I should know what that word means. "Elk."

"What?" I ask.

"You've never had jerky?" He chews laboriously, finally swallows, tears loose another bite.

I shake my head, continue to inspect the food, smell it carefully. "What is it composed of?" I ask him.

"Composed of?" He hesitates for a moment, thinking.

"It's meat. Animal muscle, from an elk. The Gelaming in Irulin smoke and season it with wild mustard and ground bladderpod. It's delicious, kinda tangy." He gestures. "Try it."

Cautiously, I put a corner of the strip in my mouth, let it settle across my tongue. The taste comes slow, rises rich and substantial, a little greasy, a little spicy. Meat, just as he says, but the diagnostics I run on it turn up no references that match the cellular structure. *Elk. Bladderpod. Wild... mustard?*

"Good, huh?" He grins around a mouthful.

It's hard to chew the jerky, but I work at it until I get enough saliva to talk again.

"Elk," I begin, and Tyse glances back at me, shoving his blankets into his pack. "What kind of animal is an elk? What does one look like?"

"I dunno." Tyse shrugs. "They look like deer, I think. Antlers." He mimes something like horns at the crown of his head, but then branching, tree-like. I'm mystified by the display. I feel like I should know the kind of animal he's talking about, but there's nothing in the reference data I carry in the silicon part of my mind that compares to it. "They eat grass and chew the leaves off trees. They range way north of here, I think. Miles."

"Elk." I nod, look at the jerky in my hands. "It's good. Thank you."

"I've been saving it for a special occasion," he says, and I can tell from the tone in his voice that he's half joking.

I chew through the jerky a little more, work toward speech again. "Special occasion?"

Tyse makes a dismissive gesture, so I let the question go. There's a tension to his movements that's subtle, barely perceptible. *He's nervous about meeting with the Gelaming,* I realize. *Has to be.*

"All packed." He zips up his bag suddenly, turns to look at me, stares as if seeing me for the first time. Rising, I look down at myself, look back at him.

"What?" I ask.

"You—you can't go into Irulin looking like *that.*" He gestures at the coat hanging from my shoulders, the total lack of any other clothing. "Here," he says, and then he's in the pack again, dragging one of the blankets out, pushing it at me. "Wrap up in this."

I wrinkle my nose at the blanket, pull the coat a little closer, shake my head.

"It's all I have besides what I'm wearing." He presses it to his face, smells it, then pushes it at me again. "It's fine. Just wrap it around you."

"Why?" I ask.

"Because your body is making me uncomfortable," he admits. "I haven't seen a woman in years, much less a naked one." He walks around the fire, holds the blanket out to me again. "It's called modesty. You're going to make a lot of hara uncomfortable if you show up in Irulin with your ass hanging out."

I wrap one hand in the blanket, draw it up against my chest. "I know what modesty is, Tyse."

Tyse says nothing, simply gestures to my chest and breathes a frustrated sigh. I watch him carefully for a moment, finally decide the best option is to cooperate. Shucking off the jacket, I wrap the blanket around my torso, tie it to the side tight enough to make it stay. It feels like a dress, kind of. A low-cut, short-hem dress of scratchy wool. I hate it. Already, I hate it, but I wear it anyway.

"We'll find something better in Irulin," Tyse says. He watches as I bend to pick up the jacket, pull it back on. "How is it?"

"Itchy." I flare my nostrils. "It has a smell."

Tyse shrugs, shoulders his pack. "Beggars can't be choosers. It'll get you to Irulin, maybe…" He shakes his head. "Yeah, you're going to stand out, no matter how you're dressed. I guess there's no getting around that."

"Maybe you should wear this blanket and I'll wear the pants," I shoot back.

"Won't make a difference." He shakes his head. "Bear with this, Vaetta. There are going to be a lot of hara interested in you when we get to Irulin, and all of them for different reasons."

"I'm not programmed for sex." I throw it out there, just cut right to the center of what I assume must be the reason for the awkwardness.

"That's not what I mean," he says. "The Gelaming are peaceful, generally, but this world isn't like the one you left behind. I've met hara who wouldn't care what you are or what you're programmed for." He swallows, seems to chew on his thoughts for a moment. "Just stay close to me. I know you can take care of yourself. Hell, you kicked my ass last night, but I know this world better than you do. I can't guarantee your safety, but maybe I can help you stay safe."

Watching him, studying his features, I decide his concern must have some merit, or at least enough to respect. At the very least, it comes from a good place, a genuine place. Tightening the knot holding the blanket-dress together, I nod, gather my empty pistol and force it through a hole torn in the lining of the coat. Tyse winces as he watches, shakes his head.

"Ready?" I ask, looking past him to the hills rising on either side of the copse.

Tyse says nothing, only sets his jaw and nods, crossing past me to make his way north, trudging uphill and through the dry grass, his clothing already collecting burrs. I linger for a moment to kick a little dirt onto the dying embers of the fire, then turn and follow him. Already, the sun is pulling loose of the horizon, brilliant and blinding. Ahead of us, the hills are shining and golden.

Tyse points at a narrow black seam cutting north and east through it all.

"Highway 88," he says. "We'll follow it, but at a distance." He glances back at me, then squints into the sky over my shoulder. "Magic can only do so much to hide us. Staying off the roads is the best way to avoid the drones, especially this close to Cinder Hill."

"Lead the way." I try a smile, find it reflected on his face right before he turns away again, nodding, silent.

CHAPTER 14

Ten miles. My mind runs the conversion, compares it to a log I'm building of the steps we take. A little over sixteen kilometers, and most of it through the dry and scratchy burr-grass. The air shimmers around us in a tight bubble as we walk—more magic, more of whatever Tyse is doing to keep the machine mind from seeing us. It's mesmerizing, gives me something to distract myself with.

Until the drones come.

"Stop," Tyse hisses, barely above a whisper. When he drops into a crouch, I follow him down. A gust rushes through the grass around us, head-height now. When he points suddenly, I see what's caught his attention, focus in on it.

I can't tell what they are at first. They're fast, streaking and wheeling across the sky like birds—but they aren't birds. Birds don't turn or bank or double-back suddenly with such speed or precision. They're machines, air-capable drones carrying the long, thin cylinders of what look like warheads—*guided weaponry.*

I try to speak, but even before I can breathe a question, Tyse puts a hand over my mouth, looks at me sternly, shakes his head. My eyes go wide, but I understand. Above us and to the east, the drones wheel and dance like hawks, hunting something, hunting us, perhaps.

I don't know how long we wait. Time passes with a tenseness I feel in my shoulders, my legs. Neither one of us moves, but we lean on each other, against each other, propping each other up until the drones fly off suddenly to the west. When they burn hard overhead, disappear beyond the horizon, Tyse breathes a sigh of relief that is deep and shivering. I take the cue, lean forward to catch his attention.

"They're looking for us, aren't they?" I ask.

He shakes his head. "There's no way to know. The Dragon is devious, hard to predict." He swallows, looks at me directly. "For all we know, this is just another play to lure us into a false sense of security, make us think we're invisible until breaking the illusion really counts."

I say nothing, only look off to the west.

When Tyse rises, he reaches for my arm, lifts me with him. "Come on," he says. "They'll be back. They always come back."

Tyse breaks into a run, sprints the rest of the way across the hills to another seam between rises, and it's everything I can do to keep up with him. Without shoes, without the cushioning light of simclothing beneath my feet, the soil is hard at best, rocky and sharp at worst. Burrs, the long spines of star thistles, jagged rocks, broken bottles—I find it all with my feet as we run, end up limping before we can even skirt past the caves, the empty center of Cinder Hill. Tyse doesn't seem to notice until we hit a trail of boards—maybe what once was a railroad—and even then, he only pauses, panting, shaking his head. Uncertain of what to do, I do my best to lock out the pain, watch him as he squats, gestures.

"Here," he says, indicating his open hands, his shoulders. "Climb on. I can carry you the rest of the way."

"It's still over ten kilometers," I remind him.

"I know." He pants, gestures again, unslinging his pack, fastening it so it sits across his chest instead of his back. "I've got this. Climb on."

It's surprising to me how easily he rises and starts

running again. He's strong, far stronger than his height and his wiry frame would seem to indicate. Curious, I reach out and explore one of his biceps with my fingers, testing the musculature, comparing it to my understanding of human physiology. The differences are subtle, slight variations in density, in tensile strength, but still prominent enough that I can feel them.

"What are you doing?" The question comes soft, curious, panted between breaths.

"Gathering data," I respond, tracing lines in the creases between muscles in his upper arm. There's a certain thrill I get touching him like this, feeling the slick sweat rising across his smooth skin, the tactile sensation, the scent of it. I can't explain it. I've never felt anything like it before, and it feels...

"Why?" he asks, bringing me back.

Hesitating for a moment, I consider his question, consider how to respond to it. *Why gather data? Because I've been programmed to like it. Because there are curious people back home who desire it. There are tactical reasons, practical reasons.*

Reasons I can't explain.

"Because," I finally say, "because I want to."

Tyse doesn't respond. His pace doesn't waver. Maybe it doesn't matter to him, maybe he doesn't really care why I gather data. Maybe he's as curious as I am, gathering his own data for his own reasons. He's an enigma to me, mysterious in so many ways, and I wonder briefly if I am at all a mystery to him, if he sees me as more than a means to an end, the evidence he needs to pit the Gelaming against the Dragon. Maybe that's all there is to it. Maybe we're only using each other.

Neither of us speaks again for a long while. Tyse is

strong, but he can only hold his pace for maybe fifteen minutes before he has to slow to a walk. Adrenaline carries him as he carries me—I can tell he's eager to pass Cinder Hill, to get into the sporadic tree cover to the east of the city center, but even Wraeththu have their limits. When he stops in the shadow of an old shack, trying to catch his breath, I offer to walk beside him again. He shakes his head at the idea, makes a weak gesture in the direction of my feet. It's kind of him, shows a level of empathy I'm unfamiliar with. I tear myself loose from him anyway, stand carefully on the dirt, trying to keep weight off the cuts and bruises.

"I have software that can lock down the pain," I tell him. "It fails intermittently because of the interference, but even when it fails, I can still walk."

He wipes sweat from his brow, pushing it into his hair. "It slows you down," he lies.

"Then heal me," I suggest. "Like you did last night."

Tyse stares at me for a long moment, as if considering, then finally shrugs. Grunting, he gestures at one of my legs, and I back up to lean against the shack, raise one foot at a time so he can work on them.

"We've got to get you some shoes in Irulin," he says, and before I can even respond, there's a heat between us, between the palms of his hands and the soles of my feet. Diagnostics register a sudden drop in pain, track the healing as it occurs. It's incredible to me, the way the glow centered in his hands stimulates the broken flesh to knit and regenerate at such an unbelievable rate. I look on as he works, parse the data and make speculations as the wounds in my feet push out dirt, seal behind shards of stone, slivers of glass, iron and wood. When it's done, I flex my toes, test everything in the dirt. Optimal, just like before, like the wounds were never even there.

"Come on," Tyse says, then turns and starts walking again. There's a slump in his shoulders now, a heaviness. Exhaustion, I'm certain of it.

Carefully, I reach out, touch his arm. "Let me carry you, now," I offer.

Tyse stops, looks at me for a moment, then shakes his head. "No. Just walk." He scrapes more sweat from his face, soaks it up with a sleeve. "I'll be fine."

"I'm stronger than I look," I tell him, but it doesn't make a difference.

Shaking his head again, he starts to walk toward the trees, eyes set firmly on the east.

I linger there by the shack, watching him for a breath or two before I hurry to catch up, walk beside him as he leads us toward the curb of a crumbling road. Briefly, I think about what Lydecker said, about the Wraeththu being hauntingly beautiful, looking like angels. Even through the dirt, the grime and the ragged clothing, I can see it now. There's something about Tyse, something about the way he moves, the sleekness of his skin, the meld of masculine and feminine traits within him, an elegance I can't deny. A mutant still, but maybe...

I kill the thought, lock it down. There's chaos in my mind, so much chaos, boiling just beneath the surface. The interplay between the animal elements of my physiology and the synthetic and silicon has been knocked out of balance by the interference and the corruption from the touch of the webs. Parts of me are fragmenting within, dropping out of harmony. It's terrifying, but also oddly thrilling. Exploring the breaks in my psyche without locking them down immediately is an indulgence, a dangerous one, but as far as I am from home, with as little hope as I have for survival...

As far as I've gone, I'll probably be repurposed if I ever get back anyway. For a moment, I imagine myself as a hero, as the one Valkyrie who single-handedly brought down the Dragon and the plague mutants, clearing the way for safe colonization. I can imagine welcoming the first settlers and scientists, being given new orders from Chief. Even in my brightest fantasies, I can't imagine those orders being anything but a complete physical and psyche evaluation, the results of which, at the level of fragmentation I'm already experiencing, would certainly recommend my destruction. Unreliable asset, they'd call me, and my final valiant act to prove them wrong would be to walk willingly into a recycling tank, let the bacterial soup embrace me, reduce me to my basest elements.

And I will do it willingly, I know. I am a tool. Following Chief's orders, no matter what they are, give me purpose.

And purpose is life.

"You're very quiet," Tyse says suddenly.

Coming back, I focus on the road, the pitted asphalt half-swallowed by brush and dead grass. We're far enough outside the city center now that Tyse feels safe taking the roads, the more direct routes. Trees rise out of the seams between hills, crowd in around us as we walk. Looking at me, Tyse tries again: "You seem lost in thought."

"I was," I say.

"What were you thinking about?"

"Purpose." I know it isn't much, but suddenly I don't feel like talking or volunteering any more information about myself.

Tyse watches me for a moment, as if he expects me to

elaborate on my thoughts. When I don't, he raises his eyebrows, sighs and turns away. We pass the next few kilometers in silence, and when we speak again, it's Tyse who breaks it.

"We're getting close," he says. "You should walk behind me." He gestures at the trees that follow the steady, sweeping curves of the road. "They'll spot us soon, if they haven't already. Let me do the talking. Irulin doesn't get many visitors who come in on foot."

"How do they normally come?" I ask, slowing to cross behind him.

Tyse doesn't answer at first, seems to take a moment to consider his words. "It's hard to explain," he finally says. "How do your people travel across continents?"

"Skytrains, skycars," I offer, trying to think of more obscure ways to travel long distances quickly. *Continents?* It says a lot about how connected the tribes are, how able they may be to respond to threats like an invading army from another Earth. Not savages, then, not completely. "Boats." I throw it out there, even knowing that most humans from my world would rather fly than spend weeks at sea.

"Nothing like..." He pauses, gestures. "Teleportation? Sci-fi, space travel stuff?"

"Teleportation?" I slow a little, have to catch up. "The Gelaming can teleport across continents?"

"No!" Tyse laughs, shaking his head. "Nothing like that, I promise."

"Then why did you mention it?" I ask.

"Because it's the closest thing I can think of to what the Gelaming *can* do." he says. "It's hard to explain. You'd have to see it."

"I'd like to." I say it hurriedly, eager to see, to

understand.

"More data gathering?" He asks, and there's a playful note to it.

"Curiosity, mostly," I answer, watching him, his features, the way he grins.

"Well, maybe if you're lucky, you'll get to see it."

"Then again," a voice breaks into the conversation from the trees, rich and regal sounding. "Perhaps not."

Tyse stops instantly.

Picking up on his tension, I drop into a shooting stance, draw the pistol and aim it directly at the source of the voice. Tyse's hand darts out before I can blink, wraps around the top of the matter weapon, pushes it down so that it's pointed at the ground.

Ahead of us, two hara seated upon great white beasts move into the road from the trees on either side. Horses, I realize after a moment. Horses, but elegant and regal, far more so than anything I've seen in old pictures. I note the white robes of the hara, their simple, silvery jewelry. Gelaming? Maybe. Their eyes are sharp and piercing, their lips bent into soft frowns as they inspect us.

"Tyse," the one closest to us says, and I can tell from his tone that any welcome we might receive will be mostly tepid, maybe even chilly. When he looks at me, his frown intensifies a little. "Is that— is that a *woman*?"

"She has important information about the Dragon," Tyse says. "She's been in the caves. She's seen what's down there." He pauses, swallows as the har looks at him again. "We need to speak to Laluinel. It's important."

"If it concerns the Dragon, it is always important," the other har says, nodding at his compatriot before turning his horse toward the road ahead. "Gleylen, escort them to the camp. I'll ride on and let the others know."

Gleylen nods, turns back to us, and the look on his face is softer now. The frown is gone. "This way," he says, gesturing as he turns his own horse away from us.

When Tyse takes the gun away from me, I let him. Without ammo, it's nothing but an empty threat. For all I know, the Gelaming can see through it as easily as Tyse did.

When I look up again, the har who left to ride ahead is gone, completely gone, and entirely without a sound. It's eerie, leaves me wondering about the Gelaming and what kinds of abilities their tribe might possess that the people of my Earth are completely unready to face in battle.

"Stay close to me," Tyse reminds me, reaching out for my hand.

When I take his in mine, I feel oddly compelled to squeeze it, end up indulging the desire just once, gently. Tyse gives a soft, reassuring squeeze back in response, and somehow, for some reason I can't understand, the action fills me with a sense of warmth, of comfort, solace.

CHAPTER 15

Gleylen's horse is quiet, unnaturally so. Even on asphalt, there's no click and clatter of hooves, only a sound so soft that it makes me uncomfortable, coming from an animal so large. As we walk, the road seems to shift at intervals, as if we're walking through the stilted frames of a corrupted data feed. It takes me a moment to realize that it isn't the road itself, or the trees or the landscape— it's something else. Illusion, more Wraeththu magic impressing itself on the animal side of my mind. Layers of optical camouflage, but coming from where?

When we reach Irulin, it comes suddenly. Trees flicker and part, shifting and phasing out of existence to open the road into the settlement. No walls, no gate, no guard towers—the whole place is an open clearing of simple buildings and elegant, white tent structures. In a way, it looks military. The few hara I can see are dressed exactly as Gleylen is, uniforms of white silk with silver adornment, some of them carrying sheathed swords, others leaning against the hafts of spears, ever watchful. True to his warning, all eyes that we cross linger on me, staring, studying, and I wonder what thoughts are moving behind all those steady gazes.

"Wait," Gleylen says. Dismounting, he leans in to whisper something into his horse's ear, and the beast seems to nod and wicker in response, as if it knows, as if it understands. When he steps away, the horse continues deeper into the settlement without him, walks steadily, silently on. When Gleylen turns to us again, I note his height, his willowy build, the military precision of his movements. He makes a solid gesture with one arm, hand knife-flat to indicate a series of tents on the far northern side of the clearing. "This way."

The course he chooses for us takes us down a softly-worn trail between a pair of simple white buildings busy with activity and the scents of cooking food. Snatches of conversation rattle from the high, open windows, and as we pass, I lock eyes with a har who seems mesmerized by me. Halfway through scrubbing a pot, he stares at me as if trying to figure out what I am, eventually abandons his brush and pot and hurls himself back inside the building, shouting something I cannot hear or understand. A moment later, the trail turns and we're behind a stand of elegant tents, but I can hear the clatter of feet at the door of the building behind us, the hushed whispers of hara curious to see the human in their midst.

Most of the hara we pass seem to know what I am, seem to know enough about humans only to eye me warily. No one stops us, no one sneers or shouts anything obscene, but the silence we receive from most of the Gelaming is almost more unnerving than any outright hostility. There is something in the eyes, something in the way they watch me, that makes me wonder how much they know, how much of my mind, my intents, my purpose they can see merely by meeting my eyes.

"Wait." Gleylin stops us just outside a tent, although to call it that does no justice to the size of the structure. A campaign tent, perhaps, all white canvas and poles, but more massive than any of the others I've seen in Irulin so far. From the outside, I can see the divisions in the design, the three wings that stretch out from a center that must be twenty meters across, but the purpose of it all eludes me. It is impressive, so much so that I wish I could flicker my clothing into something more formal, something more like a dress uniform reflecting my status among my own people, but there is no response from my emitters. The connections to the lacings in my skin have gone almost totally silent.

"Gleylin." A har pushes aside one of the flaps at the entrance to the massive tent, and I recognize him immediately as the other har from the road. "He's ready." He glances at Tyse and I, just for a moment. "Bring them in."

A nod from our escort, another gesture, and we follow him into the tent. The har at the door falls in line behind us, keeps me moving even though there's so much to look at inside that I'm almost compelled to stop and stare. Elegant silver lamps set with stained glass in brilliant hues of blue and gold hang from the towering ceiling, and in the middle of it all, a huge, mahogany war table, with a map that seems to generate its own strange points of firefly light, dominates the space. Rugs and tapestries lie and hang everywhere, brilliantly woven with threads of shining crimson gold—and then I see him. It must be him. His uniform is simple in cut but lavish in the details, in the shining silver stitching and the cobalt-colored designs cascading down the length of his white canvas sleeves. His hair is long and golden, falls beside his high, royal cheekbones and across his chest, shining at odds with his dark, tired eyes. Laluinel, the har in charge in Irulin. He has to be.

"Tyse." He says the name, and there's only a hint of warmth to it. The two hara know each other, that much is clear, but there is no animosity between them, only a wariness, maybe a sense of judgment, disdain. When his eyes meet mine, I swear that he can see within me, see every secret I hold and lay it open, completely visible. "Farim tells me you have seen what the machine mind keeps hidden in its caves. Is this true?"

"Yes," I breathe, transfixed.

"I believe you," he says, and suddenly I feel like his gaze has released me, like I am no longer held utterly in thrall to him. The smile that spreads across his face is soft, light. "My name is Laluinel. I lead the project that monitors the evolution of the machine mind. It is our duty to keep it both safe and contained while we study it." He pauses. "What shall I call you?"

"Vaetta." It spills from me immediately, and the stream that follows is enough to raise Laluinel's eyebrows slightly. "Commission number V1041 Kappa. Fifth-generation Valkyrie model. Government issue tactical and strategic analysis configuration. Currently assigned to Grey Division."

"These are words I know," he says, striding up to the edge of the war table, putting his hands on the elegantly-carved rim at the edge of the map. "In this order, as components of a designation, they come together in a way that sounds military, but unlike any military, hara or human, that I have ever been familiar with." He pauses, gestures. "Where are you from?"

"Earth," I hesitate, add: "Not this Earth. A different Earth."

"The Dragon has discovered a way to spread itself to parallel timelines," Tyse puts in suddenly, attracting Laluinel's eyes again. "It opened a Conduit to her world, her Earth, and brokered a deal with the humans there to destroy the Gelaming."

"Not to destroy," I correct him. "The Dragon asked us for assistance in defense and diplomacy against the

113

Gelaming." I pull in a deep breath, steadying myself. "It was a ruse. My entire team, fifteen Valkyries—there was a trap. I was the only one who escaped."

"This is a significant development. As such, there will obviously be a great deal to discuss." Laluinel taps his lower lip with a finger, considering, then turns to the two hara waiting patiently on either side of the only visible way in and out of the tent. "Farim, Gleylin. Send for tea and sandwiches. Clear my schedule for the rest of the day and put Heurian in charge of the reports on drone activity." He looks at me again. "I want to know everything. I want to know about your people, your world, and everything you saw in the caves beneath Cinder Hill."

I nod. "You'll have it."

"Tyse." He turns to the other har, watches him for a long moment. "If you have business in Irulin, you may leave Vaetta with me and go about it."

"If it's all the same to you," Tyse says, shifting his weight to one leg, hands going to his hips, "I'd rather stay."

Laluinel's smile cracks a little wider. "To you, this probably seems like the opportunity of a lifetime. Nothing you'd want to miss a moment of."

"When you lose your chesnari to the jaws of the Dragon," Tyse begins, his eyes sharp, as unwavering as the growl within his tone. "When you live through the slaughtering of your entire tribe and your only harling, when you watch firsthand, the rape of your home, the loss of every reason you have to continue on—then, Laluinel, you can tease me about my lust for revenge. It's the only thing I have left. It's why I survive."

"This I know about you." Laluinel raises a hand in a

gesture of peace. "No offense was intended. I apologize. I know what you've been through, and I should have been more sensitive to your pain."

"I know I'm not Gelaming," Tyse says, his growl fading, softening. "But I am har. We are all Wraeththu, all of the same blood, and the Dragon has only ever had one purpose. To eradicate us. To wipe our kind from the face of the Earth by any means necessary. It is a clear and present threat to all of us." He pauses, licks his lips. "I've been waiting *years* for you to see that."

"And perhaps tonight, I shall." Laluinel gestures to the northern wing of the tent, a side area lit with more of the elegant lamps and decorated by soft chairs and a velvet chaise. "Come. Let us talk of Vaetta's world and of the machine mind. Tea will be along shortly. Dandelion tea, if I'm not mistaken, with honey and cream, if you take it that way. We can discuss everything in comfort." His eyes flick from one to the other of us and back again. "The road has been hard for both of you, I'm certain. I'll have baths drawn for you later, and you'll dine with me when the evening meal is served."

"Thank you for your hospitality," I offer, but Laluinel waves it away with a smile.

"The Gelaming aspire to exemplify the best within all Wraeththu as a species," he says, and I can hear the genuine pride and confidence in his tone. "You are a guest, Vaetta. I want you to know the Gelaming inside and out. I want you to see that whatever lies the machine mind has told your people about us are false. I want you to see, with your own eyes, how great our civilization truly is, and how powerful an ally to your people we could come to be."

Tyse looks at me then, just for an instant, and I can see

something like fear in his eyes, worry. Suddenly the tent feels cold, alien. I force a smile, nod to Laluinel, but I swear his own smile has faded a little. Something else hides behind it. Something I cannot place or name, and I wonder, briefly, if we're all just using one another, if the price of dinner and a bath might be more than just the simple exchange of information.

"Ah, the tea has arrived." Laluinel breaks the sudden silence, brings warmth back into the room. He crosses along the opposite side of the table to meet Farim at the door to the northern wing of the tent. Taking the tray, he thanks the other har and dismisses him with a wave. Carrying the tea to a table just inside, he starts pouring cups for all of us, turns to regard me first, directly.

"How do you take your tea, my dear?" He smiles, and the curve of it is so sweet, so genuine that it almost convinces me to drop my guard. "Honey? Cream?"

"Both," I respond, never having tasted either, much less knowing what to expect the taste of tea to be like.

CHAPTER 16

For hours, we talk. I don't know whether it is the tea, or something in the way that Laluinel looks at me, but I feel like I can tell him everything. I feel so comfortable I tell him things I haven't even told Tyse. I tell him details about my daily routine, about the politics and political players of my Earth. I lay out the differences between humans and all the different varieties of labgrown servants and soldiers, even start spouting technotes and specs until he redirects me. With absolute trust, I tell him about the plan to colonize his world, to bring more of my people through the Conduit, and he nods excitedly through it all, eager and encouraging. Not once do I question why I'm telling him all this. Lost in his eyes, I can't help but trust him completely.

And the tea is delicious.

At some point, Tyse slips out of the tent, leaves me alone with the Gelaming leader. I hardly notice when he goes. I've hardly noticed the passing of time at all. There's so much to say, so much to tell Laluinel about myself and my world that I practically stumble over my own tongue trying to get it all out. Even when dinner comes, I talk through the chewing, and there are moments where feeding myself seems less important than filling Laluinel's ears with every detail of my Earth, its culture and Chief's plans for the world of the Wraeththu.

And still, long into the night, the tea keeps flowing.

It's late when it ends. I go on and on, and even as I talk, I can see something fading in Laluinel's eyes. There's a moment where it ends, which feels confusing in retrospect, a moment halfway through a sentence when Laluinel waves his hand dismissively, and suddenly I'm too shocked to speak. I can't place a reason to it, can't say what has shocked me — and then, in the space of a breath, I'm suddenly drowsy, so tired I can barely keep my eyes open. Across from me, Laluinel rises and stretches, looking off to the side for a long moment before he looks back, meets my eyes again.

"I'll have a bed prepared for you, and a bath in the morning." He looks me up and down for a moment, adds: "and clothing. You've given me a great deal to think about, Vaetta. We'll speak again tomorrow."

Yawning, it's all I can do to nod and stumble toward the entrance of the tent. I'm so inexplicably tired that I don't see Farim until he's next to me, reaching out to support me, gently taking the teacup from my hand. At my ear, he whispers something, something that doesn't make sense, but by the time I look up to ask him to repeat himself, he's gone. I wake out of what feels like a dream to find myself alone, staring at the peak of a tent from beneath the covers of a warm bedroll.

The tent is small. The canvas sides ripple in the night breezes, and beyond them I can hear the intermittent chirping of crickets. At some point, there's a whistle, keen and short, haunting, but it passes on the wind, and then I'm gone again, turning over, snuggling sideways into darkness.

I don't know for how long I sleep. The interference and corruption are so strong that even the diagnostics I run from the silicon side of my mind kick back errors and incomplete results. I feel half-aware, like I'm blinded by the loss of my digital self, forced to rely entirely on the animal elements of who I am. For the first time in my life,

I have a headache and I can't lock it away and forget about it. I'm at the mercy of my impulses, my aches. At some point after dawn, I register a feeling in my body, a sensation of restlessness, and I realize I'm tired of lying in bed.

Irulin is bustling with activity when I get up. I can't see much more than a cluster of other tents when I look past the flap of mine, but I can hear animal calls, the rattle and clang of industry, the rumble of conversation. Curious, I strip a sheet from the bedroll, wrap the soft white silk around myself and tie it off to make something like a dress. It's basic and sheer, but better than nothing, maybe.

It bothers me that I have no memory of leaving Laluinel's tent. In my entire life, I've never lost data, never blacked out or drifted from one place to another without a clear chain of readings to catalog, reference and reflect back upon. There's a moment of panic as I stand in the middle of the labyrinth of Gelaming tents, not knowing where I am within Irulin, not knowing where anything is, or even what time it is. Cut off from everything familiar, I feel utterly lost and completely alone.

"Hey," a voice comes from behind me. Turning, I find myself face-to-face with Tyse. He's so clean that it takes me a moment to recognize him. All of the dirt is gone, his rags replaced by new clothes cut from white canvas. Standing beside my tent, he looks elegant, almost blends in with the Gelaming, though there's a ruggedness to him, a roughness that makes him stand apart. He's har, as angelic as any of the others, but far more careworn and world-weary.

"Hey," I echo. Even just seeing him puts me at ease, kills most of the panic eating at the back of my mind.

Pulling in a deep breath to steady myself, I try a smile, but it falters when Tyse doesn't smile back.

"Hungry?" he asks, and I notice his arms are crossed, his stance a little stiff. Something is bothering him, keeping him distant.

"Yeah," I manage.

Tyse says nothing, only nods and gestures for me to follow him. Leaving the tangle of tents, I try not to think too much about his aloofness, the change in his demeanor, but without the software to lock down my anxiety, it starts to build again, stokes the chaos and the pain already pounding through my mind. I want to stop him, ask him what's changed, demand to know what's on his mind, but doubt and fear stop me. What if I did something, said something in the space of time I can't remember that turned him against me? What if he's decided I'm no longer useful? A thousand what-ifs tear at me—and then we're past the tents, out in the open of Irulin with a dozen hara eyeing us as they walk by.

"Here," Tyse says, reaching for me, and the feel of his warm hand in mine brings some modicum of peace to my mind. It isn't much, but it is enough. It's enough to help me find a sense of stability.

I can't help but wrap myself closer to his arm as we walk. Irulin is busy. Hara and livestock animals I cannot identify hurry from building to building, and each with such an enviable sense of purpose. There's a smell of smoke and food in the air, and as we approach the source, I marvel at the reactions it prompts from my body. The salivation, the rumbling and keenness of hunger building within me. By the time Tyse sets me down at a picnic table and places a plate of something delicious-smelling in front of me, it's too much to resist. I end up stuffing myself with so much gusto that I almost choke on the food.

"Slow down, Vaetta." Tyse reaches out, touching my shoulder, watching me with worried eyes.

Working my jaw, I try to get past the pressure in my throat so that I can eat more.

"There's plenty of food. Take small bites. There's no reason to rush."

Logically, I know he's right, but without the controls and coding of my silicon self to keep my animal mind in check, it's hard to do more than follow my impulses. Tyse, by comparison, only picks at his food, watches me with an expression somewhere between concern and wariness. Before I level out enough to do more than stuff myself and wonder what's wrong, a pair of hara cross to our table and sit down, one of them taking a seat next to Tyse, the other settling in beside me.

"Laluinel left before dawn this morning," the har closest to Tyse says, leaning in, almost whispering. His eyes are wide and soft, cornflower blue under a sheaf of wild, red-brown hair. "He took a *sedu* to Immanion. Rumor is that he's meeting with the Hegalion directly."

Tyse's expression is tight but unreadable. In the silence, the har next to him looks at me, meets my eyes evenly.

"You're Vaetta," he says. There's no doubt that everyone in Irulin knows who I am by now, so it doesn't surprise me that he knows my name. "My name is Foxlight," he offers, and I shake his hand.

"Tule Wolf." The har next to me also offers his hand and I shake it in turn. "I'm Foxlight's chesnari. We're friends of Tyse and the old Thuulhuum." He pauses, and I take in the details of his face, his long black hair tied up in a bun with two chopsticks the same shocking lapis color as his eyes. He wears makeup in the way that only women would back on my Earth, with rich lines of black sweeping into wings from his lashes towards his temples.

"Tyse has told us a lot about you," Foxlight says.

"May I touch you?" Tule Wolf asks me, and everyone looks at him. It's a strange question, but I don't see the harm in it, so I nod in response, look back to Foxlight and Tyse as the other har reaches out, rests his hand on my exposed shoulder.

"You never told me that you met my clone," Tyse half turns to Foxlight, and I can see the irritation in his eyes. "I had to hear about it from Laluinel last night, after he finished with Vaetta."

"I'm sorry, Tyse," Foxlight says. "I should have said something. The reports we made were classified as secret by order of the Hegalion itself. When we met the clone the Dragon made of you, we didn't know that it wasn't you. Even until recently there was doubt about who you were, whether or not you were the same Tyse who we met with in the caves. When we were brought in as advisers for Laluinel, part of our duty became to interact with and observe you." He glances at me, gestures. "With the appearance of Vaetta and her testimony, we know for certain now that we can trust you, that you're one of us, and not an agent of the Dragon."

"There's something here," Tule Wolf says, and all eyes are on him again. His own eyes are closed, but his hand feels warm on my shoulder, as warm as Tyse's hands felt when he healed my wounds in the night and on the road. When Tule Wolf opens his eyes, there's a light in them, intense and wondrous. "You're not like our humans," he says, and I blink in confusion, lips parting, looking for words. "There's something *in you* that is different."

"She's half machine," Tyse reminds the other har.

"It's not that." Tule Wolf shakes his head, ignoring Tyse's looks. "It's in her energy. Her *soul* is different."

"I don't have a soul," I say, and there's confusion in everyone's eyes when they look at me. "Humans have souls, and maybe hara, but not Valkyries." I pause, swallow. "I was grown in a lab. Labgrown individuals are created without souls."

"That's bullshit," Tule Wolf says, and his stare is so piercing, so stern that I have to look away. "That's something the people on your Earth told you, but it isn't true. You have a soul. I can *feel* it."

Again, I'm at a loss for words. Across from me, Foxlight hugs his arms lightly against his chest, regards his chesnari with curious eyes. "What makes her soul different from other humans?"

"Not other humans, *our humans*." Tule Wolf's eyes soften a little. "There's a level of awareness within her that I've seen in hara, but not in our humans. There's a solid core of experience and awakening related to energy work, the movement of agmara, and yet, if I remember correctly, she was astounded by your ability to heal her, Tyse."

"Her people rely on light emitters in the skin to create weaponry and clothing." Tyse gestures at me. "When she described it to me, it sounded like energy work, but like a technological equivalent. If it weren't for the effects of the Gelaming scattering field, she could probably change her appearance at will, shapeshifting by projecting and bending light itself."

"Gelaming scattering field?" I ask, glancing from Tyse to Tule Wolf and back again.

"It's one of the ways that we keep the Dragon

contained," Foxlight says. "The entire Gold Country is blanketed in an interference field that weakens the machine mind's ability to exert its influence above ground." He glances at Tyse, then turns back to me. "At first, it was completely effective. The Dragon couldn't connect with anything outside the caves, but as the machine mind has evolved to combat the field, we've had to evolve the field itself to keep the drones contained."

"It has a corrosive effect," Tyse says, staring directly at me. "I'm sorry I didn't tell you sooner. I only found out this morning."

"Corrosive effect?" There's a sinking sensation in the pit of my stomach. I have a feeling that I already know what he means, and I'm terrified of being right about it.

"The field is eating your implants," Tule Wolf says to me. "With the damage the interference has caused to the connections between your body and the machinery, the connections between your nervous system and your emitters..."

"You can fix it," I blurt out, and my eyes dart from one sad stare to another. "You can heal me, shut off the field, restore the connections..."

"We can't, Vaetta," Tyse says, and I can tell from the look in his eyes that he's telling the truth. Shocked, cold, I look at my hands, stare at them wide-eyed and sweating. Tule Wolf's touch still radiates at my shoulder, but it no longer feels wondrous. It's alien, a reminder of all that I used to have, all that I no longer have.

With no emitters, with no hope of repairing or reconnecting to my silicon side, I've been stripped of purpose.

I've been stripped of purpose, and purpose is life.

Chapter 17

I look on, dumbstruck and distant, as the three hara discuss my world, the colonization plans, the machine mind and all of the unknowns wrapped up in what the Gelaming might decide to do with the information I've given them. Tyse and Foxlight do most of the arguing, but Tule Wolf's attention keeps coming back to me. His hand never leaves my back through the whole conversation, but keeps me infused with warmth instead, anchoring me to the world, to myself. Deep within, I think I want to die. It's efficient. Without emitters, without any hope of restoring synthetic functionality, I am broken, useless to my people. Every moment I draw breath is an indulgence.

I think Tule Wolf gets a taste of the darkness within me, because at some point he interrupts the other two hara to excuse himself and I from the table. I go with him when he helps me up and leads me away, but I don't follow him out of some sense of curiosity or any genuine interest. Following him, obeying his simple instructions gives me a purpose, a small comfort, however momentary it is.

"Why do you believe that you do not have a soul?" Tule Wolf asks me as we walk.

It takes me a moment to work up an answer, to look within myself for the source of that truth. When I find it, when I find the words, the reason sounds hollow, even to me.

"It's something I've always known." I pause, then add: "It was knowledge I was programmed with."

"And who programmed you with that knowledge?" Tule Wolf asks. His tone is casual, more curious than indignant or accusing.

"It wasn't one person." I try to pin it down, but who really gave me that piece of information? A data spinner in a lab? Some faceless intern or technician who installed it as part of a massive software database package? The team of engineers, the scientists or the corporate execs who agreed that the denial of the soul should be passed down the chain to every labgrown individual like me? I shake my head, repeat the only words that make sense: "It was knowledge I was programmed with."

"It was knowledge that was included as part of an agenda," Tule Wolf points out. "The question is, do you know what that agenda was? Why would the people who programmed you teach you to deny the existence of your soul?" When I don't answer, don't even look at him, he finally volunteers his opinion. "Control. You were taught that only humans not grown in a lab have souls so that you would look up to them. You were taught that you were inferior so that you wouldn't question your role in the world that created you."

Tactically, it makes sense. As a piece of a persistent, long-term psychological cold war on an entire stratum of a society with the aim of perpetuating ease of control, it certainly seems to fit. Humans place so much importance on the soul, and as such, we Valkyries absorb some of that reverence, respect those possessed of souls all the more for something we perceive that they have innately, but which we lack.

"I want to show you something." Tule Wolf stops me, out in the open in the center of Irulin. Turning to face me, he takes my hands in his, presses our palms together and looks me right in the eyes. "Do you feel that?" he asks, and it takes me a moment to recognize what he means.

The heat—the warmth where flesh meets flesh.

"I feel your body heat," I admit.

Tule Wolf cracks the edge of a wry grin. "There's that, but I'm talking about something deeper. Do you feel that slight tingle, the pulling sensation?"

Focusing inward again, I try to find what he is talking about, the feeling in my hands. *A pulling sensation?*

And then it's there, slight but palpable, like the skin in the center of my palms is being stretched subtly. Looking up, meeting Tule Wolf's eyes again, I feel my lips part, but it takes a moment for me to find the words.

"What is *that?*" I ask.

"Your soul." Tule Wolf grins, full on. "I'm tugging at the incorporeal part of you. I'm tugging on your soul."

It's strange, even a little terrifying. As soon as I break the contact between us, the sensation is gone. Looking at my hands, I trace the lines in my left palm with a finger, trying to understand.

"What does it mean?" I ask him. "If you're right? If I have a soul?"

"It means..." He pauses, thoughtful. "It means whatever you want it to mean. It means you're not a tool to be used. You're human. It means you're just as worthy of respect as anyone else."

"I need purpose," I tell him, and there's an anxious insistence in my voice that makes me feel weak. "I need purpose to give me a reason to live."

"Life is its own purpose," he tells me, and there's a softness to his smile when he says it. "We find our own reasons for living as we go through life, as we age and mature and experience things."

There is wetness at the edges of my eyes, sudden and warm. It's confusing, something I don't understand, have no reference point for. I claw the moisture away, desperate for something to soothe my tortured heart. "The only purpose I have is to ensure the colonization of your world by the people of mine, and yet I feel as though I've gone as far as I can. I feel as though I am powerless, broken, a tool to be thrown away..."

"Vaetta," Tule Wolf takes me by the shoulders, stares into my eyes, "how do you feel about the plan to colonize this Earth?"

"I..." I struggle with the words. More moisture breaks from my eyes. There's so much chaos in me, so much conflict. I yearn for the harmony I once had, the efficiency, the balance. "I don't know. There's so much to consider if I look at it objectively, without loyalty. There are so many wonders here, so much that I worry would be destroyed, and yet there are so many people, so crowded together on my Earth."

"What do you *want*, Vaetta?" he asks me, and his words pierce right through me.

Something breaks within me then, shatters, and then I'm in his arms, trying to get as close to him as I can, trying to fill some need I can't put words to, can't understand.

"I want—I want to have a reason to live. I want to *know*. I want to know and be whole," I tell him, breathe it into the soft fabric of his robe.

Slowly, firmly, he wraps his arms around me, holds me, simply holds me. "What do you want to know?" he asks me.

"Everything," I respond, snuffling, rubbing my face against him, trying to dry my eyes. "I want to know what's right and what's wrong. I want purpose, the right purpose, a purpose that will keep me alive. I don't want to be a broken tool. I don't want to be discarded, recycled, repurposed. I want efficiency, productivity, a role as part of something good. I want to be whole."

There's more, but I can't find the words. It feels like I'm breaking down, vomiting up the chaos swirling within me.

Tule Wolf says nothing through it all, only holds me close, stroking my hair with one gentle hand. I don't know how long we stand there like that, how many hara pass by or stare. I'm not even sure if I care anymore, I'm so lost.

Eventually, Tule Wolf speaks again, and the words come soft, just above a whisper. "I want to show you something, tonight," he says, and I nod against his chest. "The people who made you, they awakened you just enough to make you useful, just enough to make you easy to control, and then they forced you into stagnation." He pauses, pulls in a deep breath. "I want to help you break past the shackles they put on your soul. Tonight, I want to awaken you to all that you are, and all you could become."

"I just want harmony, wholeness," I sputter.

"I know," he says, pressing his lips against my forehead. "I can feel the chaos in you. I can feel your soul tearing away from all the artificial supports and coding you're so used to relying on. You're lost. Tonight, I'll help you find yourself, and maybe that will bring you to balance again."

"Tonight," I whisper. "Thank you."

"We share a kinship, you and I," Tule Wolf says. "The part of you that is awakening sings to the part of me that was once human. If we were from the same Earth, I would say that we might be related, however distantly." He pauses, adds: "Perhaps it is enough to say that there is a song within your soul which I recognize, because a part of me still sings that same song."

Kinship. The concept of sharing kinship with someone human, even someone who was only once human, is jarring to me, but it also feels so exciting, strangely liberating. Rationally, I know that my biological components are distilled from human genetics, that I probably share a series of sequences derived from similar ancestry to that which produced Tule Wolf, but kinship? A sense of relatedness beyond that simple knowing bond that Valkyries share with one another—it is so new, the tip of a chain of thoughts I've never explored, or even entertained before.

"Teach me the song," is all I can think to say.

"You already know it," he says to me. Letting me go, he takes my hands in his and squeezes them. In his eyes, I can see something like appreciation, pride, a knowing kindness. It is new to me, completely alien, and yet welcome, so very welcome. "Come, let me show you Irulin. If your own tribe would kill you for being different, then maybe you can make your home here, or with one of the tribes of humans still left in the world."

Blinking, I feel the smile slowly creeping across my face. I feel as if I am standing at a door and a whole world of possibilities for life and happiness have opened before me. Nodding quickly, I find that I can't help but laugh. It comes from me loud and childlike, but I don't care. I don't care anymore.

"Life is its own purpose, Vaetta," Tule Wolf reminds me, grinning, and I know that there must be something there, something I can cling to.

Harmony, perhaps. A new sense of harmony, and a life lived free, as a human with a soul, or as something like it.

CHAPTER 18

Hope carries me through the day. The hope of harmony, the hope of a future, of feeling whole again, of realizing all that I think I can find if I only follow Tule Wolf. For hours, I give myself permission to be childlike, indulgent. Tule Wolf laughs as I discover new things, new concepts, satisfy my curiosity by asking him to explain and name whatever I can't recognize or understand. Under his guiding hand, I learn about Irulin, about the livestock, the sheep and goats the Gelaming keep, the chickens and the strange white horses they call *sedim*. With kind patience, he helps me explore and understand concepts that before were completely alien to me, concepts like sorrow and the tears that come with it, but also those more pleasurable feelings, like love, in all of its myriad, beautiful forms. Our relationship feels so natural, so close and friendly. To label him according to human terms, it almost feels like Tule Wolf could be some long lost older sibling, a sister perhaps, for all his soft strength, his gentleness, his aesthetic, even his decidedly effeminate body language.

In following him, I meet so many of the hara who make the settlement their home, learn the basic details of their lives. Even during lunch, when we stop for bowls of something called "church chowder," Tule Wolf introduces me to the domestic staff that keep the soldiers' mess warm and stocked with stew. When I venture to ask them what the chowder is made from, they laugh like they're sharing a joke with Tule Wolf. Finally he grins, and says "everything," which doesn't make for much of an answer until later. Later, he tells me the history of church chowder as a dish, describes it in detail as a poor man's stew of leftovers of every sort, all kept boiling like a porridge for days on end. "If you want something specific to eat from the mess, chances are it will cost you," he tells me, "but in Irulin, the church chowder is always free."

I nod, feeling fortunate. As far as taste goes, it's not bad. Thick and savory, even greasy, but there certainly seems to be no shortage of it.

After lunch, we meet up with Foxlight and Tyse again, find them chatting near one of the barns at the eastern end of the settlement. I don't catch much of the conversation, but it seems like it might be gossip, the latest comings and goings of Irulin. Foxlight smiles as we approach, takes Tule Wolf's hands in his and kisses his chesnari deeply, letting the moment linger while I watch and while Tyse looks away.

"Any word from Immanion?" Tule Wolf asks. It's interesting to me how he has eyes only for Foxlight, as if for a moment, nothing else around them exists.

"Laluinel hasn't returned." Tyse crosses his arms, pulls them close like he's cold.

"Where did you wander off to, my wolf?" Foxlight kisses Tule Wolf on the cheeks, lightly, playfully.

"Oh, just around Irulin." Tule Wolf takes the kisses, two or three of them, then dodges the last one with a wide grin. There's a flicker of shock on Foxlight's face when he misses, but then they're kissing again, pulling each other in, almost blending together there beside the barn. I look on in awe, my own lips moving as I analyze the movements, the change in breath, the change in heart rate, and wonder what it must be like, what it must feel like.

Intrigued, I watch until Tyse clears his throat, spits on

the grass. My eyes flick to him, and I can tell he's frustrated by the display. Almost immediately, the other two hara glance in our direction, their lips sliding apart, Tule Wolf dropping his chin, pressing his forehead against his chesnari's neck.

"Sorry." Tule Wolf is still grinning when he says it, seems undaunted by Tyse's impatient stare. "I took Vaetta to meet the others. I introduced her to some of the locals and answered questions on a few concepts she was curious about."

"I hate the silence," Tyse says suddenly. "Laluinel has been gone for hours. Gelaming bureaucracy is such bullshit."

"You can't rush big decisions," Foxlight reminds him. "The Hegalion has more than just our little corner of the world to think about, and it takes time to weigh all the options." He pauses, meets Tyse's stare evenly. "At least they're listening this time. You should relax, Tyse. Complaining won't make the wait any shorter."

"I hate being here," Tyse finally admits. Looking away, he shakes his head, makes a frustrated noise. "If he's not back by dawn, I'm leaving. The Gelaming can do what they want. This place is too... too clean, too *white* for me."

Panic sets in so suddenly that I can't stop myself from grabbing Tyse's arm. With synthetic controls gone, it takes every ounce of willpower I have to kick my wide-eyed anxiety away, even if just for an instant. "What about—what about me?" I ask.

"What about you?" He looks down at my hand, my grip on his sleeve, shakes it loose. "Your people are worse than the Gelaming. The more I think about all that you've said, the colonization plans, the disgust and disdain your people have for us..."

"Tyse," Foxlight tries, gently reaching for him.

"She calls us *plague mutants!*" he shouts. "Her people see us as defective humans, as dangerous lepers that should be killed or herded into quarantine camps so that they can 'reclaim' our lands as their own." Suddenly wild-eyed, Tyse points at Foxlight, his finger shaking. "You weren't there last night. I was. I heard everything she told Laluinel while he used that damn manipulative magic of his to drag every secret he could from her."

"I've talked with Vaetta a great deal today," Tule Wolf says, cutting Foxlight off before he can respond. "She's confused. She's new to our world and the Dragon has filled her with misconceptions…"

"How do you feel about Wraeththu, Vaetta?" Tyse looks at me directly, his eyes so piercing, voice so demanding and harsh that I can't help but look away. "Be honest. Tell us all how you feel."

I want to break. I want to break down and sob again as soon as I feel everyone's eyes upon me. I don't know what to say. I know what I've been taught, what Chief would expect me to say and believe, but if I chase the line of my experiences down to the core and try to synthesize my own opinions, I wonder if the few hara I've met is a large enough representative sample to judge all hara from. None of them seem like bad people. None of them seem any worse than the humans I've worked with on my world. I think of Tyse, I think of Lydecker, Chief, Doctor Hemmerly…

"I…" I hesitate, considering my words, trying to meet Tyse's eyes again. "I think you're imperfect. I think we're all imperfect. I think we all have incredible traits and incredible shortcomings. I think all humans, hara and labgrown individuals have that in common. Even the

Dragon is imperfect."

"How do you feel about the colonization plan you were sent here to realize?" Tule Wolf asks me.

"I feel like it is imperfect too." The words come smooth, suddenly, easily. Looking up at Tule Wolf, I start to get a grip on some of my fear, start to push forward, putting iron in my voice. "The plan as Chief has outlined it is flawed. I don't think the Wraeththu should be subjugated. I want to believe there is a way that humans and hara could live in peace, but I don't think hara should have to give up their land simply because someone else wants it." I pause, swallow. "I think there is a solution, but I don't know what it is yet."

"That's different than what you were saying last night," Tyse grumbles.

"A lot has happened since last night," I tell him. "There's a chaos within me. Controls I have relied on for my entire life have decayed and failed completely, leaving me floundering, forced to look within. I'm considering things I've never considered before today and finding my base programming is full of holes that were always there, holes I never questioned because I never needed to."

"She's going through the darkness," Tule Wolf says, and the look he gives Tyse is as pleading as it is chastizing. "She needs us now, more than ever. She knows, we know, we *all* know that her people would see her as a broken tool to be discarded, if she ever reconnected with them." Tule Wolf pauses, glances between the two other hara, then turns to me. "We're all she has. We're the only ones who can help her find herself, her true self."

"And if her true self decides that we all deserve to die

so that her people can colonize our Earth?" Tyse asks.

"That won't happen," I put in, attracting eyes again. "I don't think any of you deserve to die. I *won't* think that."

"What if the humans from your Earth come through the Conduit and try to destroy us?" Tyse asks. "Whose side will you be on then, Vaetta?"

I pause for a moment, considering. I know what Tyse wants to hear. I know what they all want to hear, and I know what Chief would want to hear. Instead of trying to appease anyone, I reach deep inside myself, gather the threads of an answer that feels right to me, give that instead.

"I won't choose a side," I tell him. "I'll work with both sides and stand between them if I have to. I'll do what I can to foster peaceful coexistence and keep the situation from devolving into a slaughter." I pause, and I can see the soft smile already forming on Tule Wolf's lips. "I don't think anyone, human or har, should have to die."

Tyse looks away, unconvinced, but as I stand there, Tule Wolf reaches out for me, takes my hand in his.

"I think that's a wise answer," he says, and the smile in his eyes is bright, full of admiration. "I can feel your conviction in your touch. You believe it. You *mean* it."

"I do." I'm barely holding myself together, standing strong only because of the absolute certainty that my stance is right, or at least as close to right as I feel like one can be.

"I don't like how quickly you've abandoned your loyalty to your people," Tyse says, eyeing me carefully. "It's hard to trust that you won't flip on us just as quickly. It makes it hard to believe you're sincere."

"She's sincere," Tule Wolf says dismissively. "Would you support anyhar who saw you as defective? As a broken tool to be destroyed?"

"If I was brainwashed, or if it was a matter of honor, the right thing to do..." Tyse cuts in.

"This isn't about honor!" I shoot back. "I'm scared, Tyse! I was built to be a tool. I was built to be loyal to my people. I'm learning new ways of looking at the world and I'm seeing that loyalty to the human race doesn't have to mean following orders without question. I'm beginning to see that humans are not the only group of people who might be worthy of loyalty and consideration. Hara are not what I thought they were. Even those in charge back on my Earth do not know the truth about Wraeththu, do not know them as I do. Maybe someday, through my eyes, they'll see, but right now they are blind and set on a course that can only bring suffering to everyone involved. I'm beginning to understand that as the true face of loyalty. Standing up and saying no to those in charge until a better way can be found."

"Revolutionary little thing." Foxlight smiles at me. "I like your idealism."

"It's not about revolution or idealism," I tell him, trying to keep the quaver out of my voice. "It's about having a worthy purpose, because I still believe that purpose is life."

"I need some time to think," Tyse says, turning away, looking toward the horizon, toward the east, as if he might run there, leave the Gold Country behind and set out for safer places in the lands beyond. Watching him, I'm sure the thought has crossed his mind before, and I wonder, briefly, what keeps him in these hills, why he stays.

When he turns and leaves, I resist the urge to reach out and stop him. I feel safe in the care of Tule Wolf and Tyse, but the trust I feel with them is still fragile and new. An odd feeling of kinship keeps me near Tule Wolf, but even still, there is a part of me that is terrified of the future, that feels lost and cold, cut off from all that I know, all that is familiar to me.

"He's been through a lot," Foxlight says to me as soon as Tyse is out of earshot.

I nod. "He used to live here." I watch Tyse walk to the far eastern end of the settlement, descend a slope toward a row of trees. "His people were slaughtered by the Dragon."

"Twice," Tule Wolf says, and there is sadness in his eyes when I turn to look at him. "We were there the second time, Foxlight and I. We saw it. We lived through it."

"And the first time?" I ask.

"The first time, only Tyse lived through it," Foxlight says. "Tyse, and a few hara who were hiding out in the deep woods." He gestures. "Let's go find a place to sit. There's still a lot about the machine mind that you don't know, things that you should know."

CHAPTER 19

For the rest of the day, I listen as Foxlight and Tule Wolf tell me about Tyse, about the Gold Country, the machine mind, and the rise and fall of the hara of the Hollow Hills as they were before the Gelaming came. Drawn in by the story, I listen in silent awe, absorbing everything I can about Cinder Hill, about Irulin when it was still called Segerstrom Ranch, and about the hara who called all of the disconnected settlements of the area home. In vivid detail, Tule Wolf and Foxlight weave an image of Tyse for me that is much deeper and richer than anything Tyse himself has told me, in any of the forms of him I've encountered. I learn about Tyse's life before the machine mind came to the Gold Country, how he was the one who saw the fallen star that the rogue human AI rode to the bottom of the great Central Valley Sea, how he was there as the rogue AI built itself up, how he and his lover Stoff were the ones who defeated it in its lair in Cinder Hill, and even then only at great cost to them both.

It hurts to hear about Stoff's death. It hurts to hear about how close they were, about Tyse's broken attempts to live with the loss of his closest friend, his mate and confidant. Their offspring—their *harling*, Cougar—neither Foxlight or Tule Wolf can tell me much about him that isn't second hand from Tyse. They barely knew him, had met him only briefly before he was taken by the machine mind after it was resurrected by the power-hungry tribal har who was the first victim it chose to devour.

Foxlight recounts that whole night with such intensity that I feel an echo of the tightness that he must have felt in his gut when the gang of highway hara, stitched with filaments of mind-controlling silicon, raided Segerstrom Ranch and dragged dozens of screaming, thrashing hara away into the night to be devoured by the Dragon, Cougar among them. I listen, and I begin to see how deeply the pain in Tyse must run, why he acts as he does, what he must feel whenever he even so much as thinks about the Dragon. He lives within a shroud of pain, and it hurts to think how much it has consumed him, how much it has colored his own soul with hate. Over and over again, I find myself wishing I could free him somehow, make his pain my purpose and cleanse him of it, but I know that it is probably beyond me, far beyond my ability. Perhaps, once a truce is brokered between the Gelaming and my own people, perhaps, once life calms and I finally find the time to settle down and explore the richness of purpose Tule Wolf seems to see within life, I can try to help Tyse with his pain, even if only just a little.

The day wears on, and Tule Wolf starts to talk about the distant birth of the rogue human AI that became the Dragon, the origin of it all. Tule Wolf's knowledge of the Dragon's past is stunningly detailed, and so in depth that I begin to wonder if maybe he was there through it all, watching the programmer who created the code purposely designed to hate all Wraeththu. When I ask him how he knows all that he does, though, he only gives me a dismissive gesture, answers with a simple "I'll show you later."

Later doesn't come soon enough for me. Even as drawn as I am into the stories that Tule Wolf and Foxlight tell, I still find myself wondering what wonders they are holding back from me, what the descent of the sun has to do with the realizations. It seems so arbitrary, having to wait until night for some revelation that Tule Wolf feels the need to drag out, but I also trust him. I trust that he has a reason, some reason that I will see as clearly as he does when the time is right.

I start to get anxious when the sun sets and Tule Wolf's only concern seems to be supper. I try not to clench my teeth at the way he and Foxlight play, teasing and kissing even through the meal, seemingly without a care.

Less hungry than frustrated, I start to wonder where Tyse is, if he's coming back, or if he's left Irulin for the hills, struck out on his own again. Being alone, I can't say I blame him. I don't like waiting for bureaucracy any more than he does.

Absently, I poke at the meal I've been given. It's simple, a salad of the last of the season's highway greens, miner's lettuce and boiled milk thistle topped with a small cut of roasted goat and the drippings as dressing. When someone places a small wooden goblet in front of me and asks me whether I'd prefer water or some of the dark, heady mead that's going around, I hesitate, finally ask for the mead. I've never consumed alcohol before, and I'm curious to see how the biological elements of my physiology deal with even a small amount of it.

When I drink, I do so in sips, weathering the burn, the harshness and the sweetness. Reaching for that silicon side of myself, I try to break down the constituents, study and analyze the elements of the mead, but everything digital within me has gone silent. The only senses I have to work with now are the imprecise animal ones that seem able only to group things into basic categories like sweet, hot and sour.

At some point, I realize that my goblet is empty. Peering into it, I try to remember where the mead has gone, wonder if I'm the one who drank it all. I look up at Foxlight and Tule Wolf and catch them laughing, red-faced and drunk, and I wonder if maybe one of them switched their goblet with mine when I wasn't looking. I barely have time to wonder, to get irritated, when someone comes and refills my cup. I glance back at the har with the mead as he slips away, but all I register in the shadows is a cascade of blonde hair and the sharp crescent of a grin.

A handful of paces away, another har takes up some kind of stringed instrument and begins to sing. The sound is even more intoxicating than the mead. His voice is rich and smooth in the same way that honey and velvet are, and his red-gold ringlets roll down the front of his green tabard as he smiles at me, seems to be singing to me. Squinting, I try to focus on the words of the song, interpret them, parse them into something understandable, but nothing comes to me. He's singing about love, life, and honey. That much I can tell, but the rest is lost, as if whispered in a dream.

And then there is a moment that unfolds soft, surreal in its suddenness. One instant, I'm listening to the music, watching Foxlight and Tule Wolf in their romantic play, following their little kisses, the way their fingers move in an interlacing dance. The next, it's my hand dancing with Tule Wolf's, interlacing, and the smile on his face is full of love.

It takes me a moment to register that Foxlight is gone. Even the singing har is gone. We're alone, and as Tule Wolf takes my hand in his, I swear that I can see summer storms reflected in his cobalt eyes, the flash of lightning across a boiling sky. My heart freezes beneath the intensity of his stare, and in the pause, I hear a whistle, the same haunting whistle I heard the night before.

"What is that?" I ask.

"Mountain lion," Tule Wolf says and, as his lips part over sharp and perfect teeth, I see the sky in his eyes flash. There's a sound then, not a whistle, but a cry, blood-chilling and shrieking harsh, a call that cuts the air far in the distance. Tule Wolf's eyes fill my soul, possess me utterly, and then he says: "she calls."

I want to ask him what a mountain lion is. I want to ask him about the cry and the whistle. The sound is so powerful, so primal. I want to ask him so many questions, but he tugs at my hand before I can speak, pulls me to my feet and urges me to follow him instead.

Irulin is unnaturally silent as we steal our way toward the trees at the far eastern end of the settlement. A slight breeze ripples across the canvas of tents, tugs at my arms and legs with frigid fingers. The moon is full and bright overhead, throwing a silvery glow over everything. When we run, we run with a building, spreading speed that seems impossible. When we reach the forest, suddenly it is beneath us, as if we're running so fast that we're flying, *flying*.

And then Tule Wolf leans in with a mischievous grin, whispers a word in my ear that I recognize, that unpacks a whole other world of data in my mind.

"*Valkyrie.*"

My wings are huge and gray, beating at the night, and ahead of us, the moon is a well, deep and stirring with the movements of a mated pair of primal swans. *The well of Urd*, someone says, and with it comes a flood of images. The moon, the moon as a place, as a rocky sphere tidally locked with Earth, but also as a window to a greater realm, a well upon rich, black soil studded with flakes of shining snow. A well far above and also below us, a window into fate.

Fly, Valkyrie, someone says, and I do.

"We share a kinship," Tule Wolf says, breathing the words from just over my shoulder as we ascend toward the great well of fate. "The part of me that was human sings the song that your blood sings, that your soul sings." He points at the stars, the sprawling, shining swathe of the galactic plane cutting across the sky, rooted in the south, rooted in the moon and in other wells that stir somewhere in the darkness beyond my ability to see. "Do you see it? Do you see the mighty ash tree showered in shining white hail?" He jabs his finger into the rushing wind, tracing lines in the stars to show me the great tree— and then I see it. Overlaid upon the milky way itself, the great tree, and Tule Wolf breathes its name: "Yggdrasil!"

I do not ask how I know these things, how Tule Wolf knows these things. The tree, the moon—it defies rational comprehension, and yet it is there, it is all there, and the words flow into me like a stream, filling me with lore and images and such sights as I have never seen through augmented eyes before. Within the stars themselves there are symbols, alien and yet familiar, symbols that sing a song that roars within my blood, but also within my soul, *my soul!*

I cry out as tears stream from my eyes. *My soul! My soul!* I am not a tool. I am human, alive and possessed of a soul.

Tule Wolf laughs as I scream to the heavens, to the well and the stars. "I have a soul!" I yell, and in the night something parts, something like a great veil speckled with snow, and then a great force reaches through, seizes my heart and fills me with a challenge I cannot refuse.

Valkyrie! Yes, you have a soul.
Are you ready to use it?

"Othinn!" Tule Wolf howls to the great force, spreading his arms wide, his wings open, so huge that they seem to stretch from horizon to horizon. His streaming cascade of midnight hair flies out like a banner in the wind, mingling with mine, and I swear in that moment that Tule Wolf himself is my soul, or that we share a soul, that we are one, or that he is the embodiment of all that I could become. Together, we sing to the spirit in the stars, and like the skywide manifestation of some eternal father, the spirit sings back.

The song is sweet. It burns like fire, like the bite of mead, and as we follow it, I swear it is leading us into the eternal night, to a single shining point, a star that glitters and winks like a solitary eye amidst the blackness. Soaring, tireless, I look for Tule Wolf, look for my friend, my kin, my brother-sister, only to realize that we are one, that I am Tule Wolf, that my wings are his, and all that I am I share with him.

The star grows suddenly as we approach, becomes a great island floating in the sky, a craggy land supported by one of the great starry limbs of the eternal tree. Gliding in, I follow the song of Othinn as if I know the way, as if I've been to this impossible place before, as if I'm coming home. Other shapes rise from trees to greet me, and at first I think they are birds, great ravens with black wings as wide as mine. Only as they come closer do I see what they really are. They are Valkyries, my sisters, and they rise to fly beside me like a radiant rainbow of colors, with every hue I've ever seen represented in skin, hair and eyes. No two are the same, and they all smile as if they know me, like they're welcoming me back, grateful to see me after a long time spent away.

"Sister Wolf," one whispers in my ear. "Othinn waits. He has seen what is within you. He has seen your soul and has wisdom for you." I look at her and she grins back, sharp and feral. She's a thousand shades of carmine, with shimmering skin and hair like flame, and I can't help but marvel at her. "Come," she says, and takes my hand in hers. Her touch is warm, and within that warmth, there is that familiar feeling of kinship again, of a bond that goes deep, deeper than the flesh, a bond between souls that sing the same song.

Like a great army, we descend upon the island from the skies, and I think for a moment that there are so many of us that surely we must blot out the sky with our approach. Below us, in the midst of a great green field of lush grass sits a huge building, a long, multi-story structure that must be over a hundred and fifty meters long. It looks old, even ancient, but also regal, as if it has been diligently cared for over the course of centuries. Even the thatch on the roof shines as if it were laid only yesterday.

I take in the great hall as we land, settling into the ankle-deep grass, and again I'm struck by the feeling of coming home. The song is loud within me, pulses through my blood, follows the rhythm of my heart, and as I stride confidently toward the source of the song, two Valkyries with deeply olive skin and shining black hair run ahead of me to open the huge, oaken doors. There is an electric hum of excitement in the air, and celebration, and then I mount the weathered stone steps, cross the threshold, and everything changes.

The huge dining tables are silent. The doors behind me are closed, barred with a stout beam, and everything in the great hall has an air of solemnity to it. For the first time since I have arrived, I am alone, and although the song still runs through my blood, I cannot hear it. There is silence, only silence.

At the far end of the hall, I see two figures watching me, waiting for me on either side of a great golden throne. As I approach, I start to pick out details, the hoary, bearded face of one and the sleek shine of the other. I know them both, somehow, know even their names, as if I've met them before.

And somehow, I know that I have.

"Wolf," the sleek one says, and as he turns to regard me, I can see the light and love in his smile. He is har, no doubt about it, and yet he is also more, so much more. Brilliantly crimson hair spills out around him, runs in glittering waves down his bare and hairless chest, and the nails of the hand he beckons me with are long and scarlet. Even the sarong tied at his waist is all shades of crimson and gold, the stitching so elegant, so precise, twisting into lines that seem to spiral into infinity in the fabric.

The old human at his side is a stark contrast to the har, stands hunched against a gnarled staff, his clothing weather-beaten, all shades of brown and gray. His wild, white-silver beard and the deep, ragged scar over the socket where one of his eyes must once have been make him look ancient, and yet there is youth and strength in his hands, a mischievous shine in his one remaining ice-blue eye.

"Othinn, Aghama." I regard them each in turn. I know whose hall I stand in, but I also know who holds sway over the domain of Earth, whose children are the most numerous. Stepping up to stand with them, I know I am in the presence of divinity, but I also know better than to bow to either. I am welcome, expected. More, I am wanted. I have purpose, and purpose, even here, is life.

"Do you know who you are?" Othinn asks me, and his voice seems to reverberate through my entire being. Even as he asks it, I know somehow that he already has the answer, that there are levels to his question, and it exists only to awaken the wisdom within me.

"I am a Valkyrie," I answer.

"You are more than that," the Aghama says, offering his hand. When I take it, I feel that familiar warmth, the warmth I felt in the hand of the Valkyrie with the flaming hair, and I wonder what secrets that similarity of soul holds. "We share a kinship, you and I."

"Tule Wolf is har." I soak in the feeling, have to resist the urge to be swept away by it, become one with it and disappear in a tide of light and love. "I am a Valkyrie. I am human."

"You were not always," Othinn says, and I see a slight curve to the edge of his lips. "You are not entirely what you think you are, Wolf."

"Are you not also Tule Wolf?" the Aghama asks. "There is division between you, yes. There is time and the tinkering of machines to separate you, but are you not still the same being?"

"I know that we share a kinship," I answer. "I feel a strong bond with him, stronger than I have ever felt with anyone else."

"There is no bond stronger than the one that Vaetta and Tule Wolf share," Othinn affirms. "You will see, in time. The strongest illusions of who you are still nest within your head. They are as strong as steel and will not yield until the right knife comes to cleave them from you."

"Do you carry that knife?" I ask him, but he doesn't answer. Even the Aghama is silent when I look at him. When my eyes eventually go back to Othinn's, I breathe a quiet sigh of frustration. "You speak in riddles, old one."

"As I have always done," Othinn says. "True wisdom comes at a price. Clarity and understanding, the ability to grip hidden concepts firmly only ever comes from sacrifice, from reaching into the darkness and tearing the runes of realization from the depths, amidst a storm of screaming and blood."

"What sacrifice would you ask me to make for clarity?" I ask him.

"Careful." He taps the scar over his missing eye. "I was as eager as you once."

"Would you take my eye?" I step toward him, but he only smiles wider. "Would you take something more?"

"I am not the one to whom you must offer sacrifice," Othinn says, then gestures at the Aghama. "Neither is he. To truly see, you must do as I did. You must make of yourself a sacrifice to yourself."

"And what will I see when I do?" I ask.

"Everything," Othinn says. "Just as I do."

CHAPTER 20

"Vaetta." It comes soft at first, a whisper out of the darkness. "Vaetta."

I jolt upright the instant I feel hands on my arm, my shoulder. There's a sound, half-formed, and then I see Tule Wolf leaning in, a look of concern on his face.

"Hey," he says. "It's okay. It's okay. You were dreaming."

"Dreaming?" I ask. Rubbing at my eyes, I try to recall how I got back to Irulin, wonder if I ever even left. The hall, the Aghama and Othinn—they were both so real. They had such *presence*. "I've never had a dream before."

"It looked like a pretty intense one." Tule Wolf strokes my hair, absently picks at some of the knots there. "You alright?"

"I saw Othinn, and the Aghama." I look up at him, meet his eyes. "I knew who they were, and they knew me."

I feel Tule Wolf's fingers hesitate in their picking and know instantly I've struck a chord with him. Almost without missing a beat, he says "What else did you see?"

Dimly, I'm aware of Foxlight sitting across from me, watching Tule Wolf and I, as I retell the dream just as it came, from beginning to end. Tule Wolf sits down next to me in silence as I speak, his hand settling on my back. The gesture is kind, is supposed to be comforting, but I can tell through his touch that some of the images and the names within my dream reach him deeply, deep enough to make him shake. When I finish telling of the Aghama and of Othinn, Tule Wolf turns to Foxlight, and something passes between them, something that makes Foxlight shiver.

"I thought we were done with gods," Foxlight says.

"The Aghama has had a hand in all of this since the beginning," Tule Wolf says. "There's no reason to believe his level of involvement would change now."

"But why Vaetta?" Foxlight asks. "How is she connected to you?" He gestures. "To all this?"

"Things like this have happened before," Tule Wolf says. As he talks, he stares off into the distance, deep in thought. "Tyse had a vision of the Aghama here before, as have I. In both cases, the Aghama brought revelations, clarity, focus." He pauses for a moment, looks at me. "It troubles me that he did not reveal more. It troubles me that it was mostly Othinn who spoke, and that everything he said came in riddles."

"Vaetta is human," Foxlight says. "The other riddles, the connection you two share—I can't even begin to guess at the meaning of that, but it makes sense to me that a human would find more connection with a human god."

"What do you know of Othinn?" I ask Tule Wolf.

"Plenty." He glances at me. "As a human child, I grew up on the stories of my ancient ancestors. They were like fairy tales to me then, but…" He shakes his head. "Othinn is wise, but he is also a trickster. He hides things and, as he said himself, he tends to speak in riddles."

"I knew nothing of him before tonight," I admit, staring off to the east, in the direction in which we flew in the dream. "Is that what dreams are? Is this how they work?"

"It is how visions work," Foxlight says, reaching for his goblet and swirling the mead at the bottom of the cup. "What you saw may have been a dream, but it was also a vision. You spoke with divine forces, that much can be said for certain, and they gave you information, however cryptic it may be."

"Does this happen to you every night?" I ask, bewildered.

"Not every night." Tule Wolf rests his hand on my back again. "And most dreams we have, even the dreams that hara have, are only the spinnings of a tired mind, a recycled pastiche of elements from the day."

I think about his words for a moment, but the images from the vision still pull at me, pull at me so strongly that it almost feels like they could take me back there, back to that great hall. I close my eyes in the moment, wishing that I could return, wishing I could learn more, find clarity in the riddles of Othinn and finally see all that he sees.

"Tule Wolf." I turn to the har, meet his eyes evenly. "With your knowledge of Othinn, what do you think he means when he says I must sacrifice myself to myself if I want to truly see?"

"I don't know," Tule Wolf says. "The only time I've heard those words used in that order, it referred to how he hung himself upon a tree for nine nights in order to receive sacred wisdom. A purification ritual of pain to loosen the bonds that root the mind in this world, in the mundane." He looks at me, seems to stare into me for a long moment, as if considering his words. "I hope that's not what he has in mind."

"Seems extreme, even for a human deity." Foxlight rests his chin in his palm, regards us both with placid eyes.

"That was the point," Tule Wolf says. "The humans who originally revered Othinn and saw him as kin were an intense and hardy people. You can still see it in the hara that sprang from those roots— the Freyhella. Othinn was the king of their old gods. He had to be tough enough and intense enough to earn their reverence."

"How do we find out what Othinn has in mind for me?" I ask.

"I have an idea," Tule Wolf says, standing. "We should find Tyse. I promised I would show you how I know the things I do, but it looks like Othinn beat me to it."

"What do you mean?" I ask, also getting to my feet.

In the pause, Tule Wolf takes my hands, smiles softly. "I mean, we should seek a vision. A new vision." He pauses, squeezes my hands. "Perhaps we can find some clarity together. Maybe that's what Othinn and the Aghama had in mind all along. A collaboration. A joint venture between a human and a har to pull some new and sacred wisdom from the very fabric of the universe."

"What do we need Tyse for?" Foxlight asks.

"There's a bond between him and the Gold Country," Tule Wolf says. "It's strong. When I had my vision, he was there, in it. We're connected, all of us, and if we're going to seek a vision here, in this place, he should be a part of it."

"I'll go look for him," I offer.

Tule Wolf shakes his head, crosses to Foxlight and takes the other har's hands in his own. "We'll all go look for him," Tule Wolf says. "I have a feeling that there's wisdom for all of us in the woods tonight."

As if in answer, I hear the call of a cougar, and my skin prickles.

Tule Wolf smiles, gestures toward the sound. "These hills have their own spirits," he says. "They take many forms, and she is one of them. I take it as a good omen, a blessing that she is in the woods now. That spirit has always been on our side."

CHAPTER 21

We find Tyse right where Tule Wolf expects him to be. Alone, crouching by the creek at the far eastern end of Irulin, he doesn't rise or look up as we approach, but I can tell by the smell of the skunky weed in his joint that it's him. Only when Tule Wolf rests a hand on his back does he seem to notice us, and even then he does not rise. One hand carries the joint away from his lips, offers it to Tule Wolf, and the other har accepts it, puffs on it in the silence that follows.

Tule Wolf is the first to speak. "We need your help."

"I know," Tyse says. "I heard her, in the woods." He gestures, and I know he means the cougar, the mountain lion. "She's been calling all night. It's happening again, just like before."

"Vaetta has had a vision of the Aghama," Tule Wolf says, handing the joint back. The lit end glows cherry red as Tyse pulls in a long draw, holds it thoughtfully before letting it out again.

"Yeah," is all he says, as if he knows, somehow.

"Come with us to the woods." Tule Wolf crouches down beside Tyse, leans toward him, their shoulders touching. "If the lion has wisdom for us, we should answer the call. We should seek our own vision, our own answers. All of us, together."

"You're right," Tyse says, stubbing the joint out in the rocks on the shore. When he stands, he shivers, and I can see his breath in the moonlight. His eyes meet mine in the pause, and suddenly he looks ancient, as ancient as Othinn, and even more world-weary, somehow. "What are you hoping to find, human from another world?"

"Clarity," I answer softly. "Wholeness."

Tyse smiles, or maybe it's a grimace. There's pain in it, irony, the seeds of angry laughter. I don't know what to make of it, wonder what he's thinking, what he's holding back. When he speaks again, he only says. "Yeah, okay. Let's go."

I stay close to Tule Wolf and Foxlight as Tyse leads us into the woods, into the trees and over animal paths that wind and crawl through the brush, the sharp, low-hanging branches. No one asks where we're going, but I swear that Tule Wolf knows the way as keenly as Tyse does. When we finally emerge into a clearing of soft, lush grass ringed by a wall of oak, cedar and sugarpine, it feels like we're a million miles away from Irulin. I look back, but there's nothing, not even a subtle glow to indicate the direction home.

"She's not here," Tyse says.

I watch him as he walks to the center of the clearing, peers up at the moon and blinks against the brightness. Beside me, Tule Wolf looks around, spots a stone fire-pit a handful of paces beyond Tyse, then crosses over to it. In the pause, I glance at Foxlight, find no reassurance, no confusion, nothing but a quiet openness to whatever is about to come.

"There's wood," Tule Wolf says, bending down next to the little ring of stones. He reaches into the darkness, shifting something there. "It's burnt, just a little." He looks up, arms across his knees. "Someone was here. Not recently, but there was."

"The pit is new," Tyse points out, turning back to look at Tule Wolf.

"You haven't been out here in years," Tule Wolf reminds him. "Neither of us have."

"You think it was one of the Gelaming?" Tyse crosses to the pit, stops as Tule Wolf stands. "Someone else the lion drew to this place?"

"Hard to say." The other har shakes his head, then asks: "should we take it as an invitation?"

"Mountain lions are afraid of fire," Tyse says.

"And spirits are called out of the darkness by it," Tule Wolf muses, smiling softly.

Instead of saying anything in response, Tyse only gestures at the stones and the wood within.

I watch in silence as Tule Wolf brings the fire to life with the heat of his hands. It doesn't take long for the wood to catch, and when the flames begin to burn with their own heat, Tule Wolf drops back into a sitting position, crosses his legs.

"Have you been a part of a guided meditation before?" Tule Wolf asks me.

I think back, but there's nothing in my memory that fits those words. The concept seems incongruous, alien. I shake my head, and he gestures to a spot on the other side of the fire. "Join me," he says, smiling.

When I sit in the grass across from him, I cross my legs in the same way that he does, study his posture and try to imitate it. When he closes his eyes, I watch him, try to match everything, right down to his heart rate, his breathing, until he says: "Relax Vaetta. Close your eyes."

It takes me a moment to break from the rhythm. I pull in a deep breath, and as I close my eyes, I let myself drift into the darkness around us. When Tule Wolf starts to speak again, the words come slow, rise from somewhere deep within his chest. They nest in the mind as they reach me, fill me with images that blossom in the darkness. I can see the light of my spirit, my soul as he describes it, and it excites me. The light, the way it moves and blooms with each inhale, expands and spreads with each exhale. His words are hypnotic, they carry me deeper and deeper, like a rope, a silver cord to climb down, down into the darkness.

And then suddenly, there is silence.

It comes like a break in the flow of time, as if it has always been there, like it is only me who has changed from a frequency of sound to one of nothingness. Echoes of Tule Wolf's voice still reverberate through me, seem to come from within me, as if it were my voice all along.

Curious, I open my eyes, expecting to see Tule Wolf sitting across the fire from me, Tyse and Foxlight pacing at the edge of the clearing. Instead, I see nothing, no one. A cool breeze stirs the grass in the clearing. Even the fire has gone cold.

"Sister Wolf." I hear Othinn's voice rumbling from somewhere among the trees, catching on the wind, as if the god is everywhere and nowhere, all at once.

I rise to my feet. "I've come for guidance." My eyes search the clearing around me, turn up nothing but the ripple of a breeze through the grass. "I want to speak to the Aghama. I want to know what I must do to achieve clarity."

"All clarity comes with time, with sacrifices yet to be made," the Aghama says, his silken voice catching my ear from behind. Turning, I find him standing only a pace or two from my back, his hands knitted together. "You want to know how you and Tule Wolf are connected, I know. That will require sacrifice, a sacrifice of yourself to yourself, but that sacrifice will not be made here. That sacrifice has already been arranged. It will come in time, and if I say more now, then you will not have the strength you will need to face the giants, the primal forces within and without you, which you must challenge to truly know Tule Wolf, and in the process, to truly know yourself.

"You speak in riddles." I shake my head. "What clarity can you give me here and now?"

"What do you see when you look at the stars?" he asks, pointing.

Following his finger, my eyes find the Milky Way spread out above us again, bright and brilliant. "I see worlds, other suns, distant from ours."

"And?" he prompts me. "What else do you see?"

I look again, and after a moment, I realize what he means, what he's talking about. "And I see the tree. I see Yggdrasil, the great ash."

"Othinn hung himself there for nine nights to learn the wisdom and the way of the magical tools that would become his most remembered contribution to the tribes of your ancestors."

The Aghama looks at me then, and in his eyes I see a firelight reflection of myself as I could be, as a Valkyrie and a master of light. Not as I was, with projected combat armor, a lightrifle and simclothing, but as something more, something brighter, more primal. The emitters in my skin are dead, and yet the connections within my soul are eternal. The runes and marks on my spirit are alive, ready to spin light in ways my emitters never could have.

"What would you do to earn your own tools, Valkyrie?" he asks. "Would you hang there in the shining hail of the great ash? Would you hang for nine days without food or water?"

"No human could survive that," I tell him.

"This part of you is not human." He reaches out and pulls at my clothing. "Time does not flow here as it flows in the mundane world. A year might be lived in a single second, or a second stretch to fill a year."

"And so nine days might pass in the space of a single breath." I nod. "In the mundane world, my body is safe, but here…" I let the sentence trail off.

"Here," Othinn's voice rises into the silence, finishing where I left off, "you place far more than your body in peril when you hang from the tree, when you look into the darkness and reach for the secrets hidden there."

"I am willing to brave it," I tell him.

"What do you believe you will gain by it?" Othinn asks, regarding me carefully with his one good eye. "Do you believe that knowledge, that the playthings of magic and spirit will bring you peace? Glory? Joy?"

"No." I pull in a deep breath, try to keep the iron in my voice. His visage is gnarled and terrible, the shine in his eye glittering, intense. "I know such things are earned. What I've seen, what I could become, the tools within me—they are only tools, I know that. Knowledge brings perspective, not peace. Glory does not come from the tools one carries, it comes from the actions and patience of the one who wields those tools."

"And joy?" the Aghama asks.

"Joy is something we choose," I tell him, and I wonder where the words come from. There is wisdom within them, but it does not feel as if it derives from the part of me that is Vaetta. It seems to come from somewhere else, somewhere deeper.

"You are ready," Othinn says, and as I look at him again, he throws out an arm, holds it with the palm up.

Light gathers in his hand, spinning faster and faster until it finally explodes into the shape of a great spear, long and blindingly bright. At the head of the spear, strange shapes glow in lines of liquid crimson, and I know then that they are runes, the mark of Othinn's power. "This is Gungnir, my spear. Even thrown, it cannot miss its mark." He pushes it at me. "It is yours, now. Take it."

Othinn watches me in silence. I try not to hesitate, but the spear is so otherworldly that I cannot help but stare. The haft, the head—the whole thing seems as if it were carved from the very stuff of the sun itself. When I close my hand across it, I'm surprised by how solid it feels, the subtle warmth within it.

And then I hear voices, the song of distant crickets. Othinn is gone, and in his place I see Tule Wolf standing with his mouth agape, his eyes wide. In my hands, Gungnir is the same as it was in Othinn's hands, sun-bright and shining, lighting up the whole clearing with a steady, constant glow. A dozen paces away, Tyse and Foxlight watch in silence, as if waiting for someone else to speak.

You are ready, I hear Othinn's voice in my mind again. *Look within, and grasp what waits to be known.*

And I do. Closing my eyes, I find a light inside, a shimmering star of stagnant fire and thunder. Reaching for it, reaching on some level beyond the physical, I seize it and tear it open, releasing everything within.

And then suddenly, I understand.

"Vaetta..." Tule Wolf takes a tentative step toward me.

I can feel it, feel all of them, the clearing, the trees and the grass and the insects all around me. With it comes an incredible sense of peace. I am whole again. I am whole in ways I have never been whole before, or at least in any way that I can remember.

I open my eyes. "I understand."

The three hara watch in wonder as I summon a wind of wild light, a vortex of rays and stars that settles into the fabric of the soft white Gelaming robes I'm wearing, transforms everything into armor, a suit of chain and plates engraved with runes I cannot name, but know the power of somehow, innately. Light flares in the palm of my free hand to become an ornate shield gilded with a pair of woven, knotwork ravens, and at my back, shimmering rays rise to become wings, solidify into the gray shades I remember from my dream. My hair flares and lifts, then falls across my back again, sleek and even. For the first time since I arrived, all of the knots in my mane are gone.

"Your emitters?" Foxlight asks, closing some of the distance between himself and his chesnari.

"No," Tyse says, and I can see in his eyes that he understands as well. "The emitters were a crutch." He looks me in the eyes. "The emitters were a crutch for you all along, weren't they? Like—like training wheels. Nothing more."

"I never knew, until now." I shake my head, and the light around me solidifies, turns silvery, metallic, no longer bright or blinding. "You saw it, Tule Wolf." I turn to regard him. "You said that the people who made me awakened me just enough to make me useful, and then they forced me into stagnation." I pause, and a smile starts to spread across my face. "I am no longer stagnant. I am awake. *I understand.*"

"And the sacrifice?" Tule Wolf asks.

Before I can answer, Othinn's voice reaches out from the darkness within me, and the tone of it, the sensation of what it might still portend is enough to make me shiver.

All things come in their right time.

I dodge the question. "Let's head back."

Tyse and Foxlight look at each other, but no one says anything, not even Tule Wolf. They only watch as I let the light go, let the armor and the wings fade back to the simple white robes I'm wearing underneath everything.

Tule Wolf puts out the fire, and then Tyse leads us back to the trails that will carry us to the light of the settlement again.

On the walk to Irulin, I try not to think too much about Othinn's words. I try not to think about what they mean, about what sacrifices he and the Aghama see that are still to come.

Chapter 22

The moment that we reach Irulin, I can tell something is wrong.

Tyse and Tule Wolf glance at each other as if they sense it too. There's noise, the murmur of excited conversation. It's late, only hours before dawn, and someone is rousing the Gelaming from their beds.

There's a noticeable increase in Tyse's pace as we cross the creek, pass the barn and the outlying buildings of the settlement. Something within him is expecting the worst. I can see it in the set of his shoulders, the tense lines of his muscles as he moves. Jogging to keep up with him, I remember Tule Wolf and Foxlight's stories, their tales of the explosive events and loss that always seemed to follow a vision of the Aghama. There's sweat on Tule Wolf's skin, glistening, and then something happens that halts me, roots me to the ground immediately.

A flash of light, bright and brilliant, with a crack like a lightning strike, and suddenly there's a horse between us, huge and brilliantly white, flying out of nothingness and touching down on the soft grass with silent hooves.

The sound I make is sharp, startled, loud enough that the silver-helmed Gelaming riding the horse looks at me as he passes, and I swear that I see a trace of disdain in his soft, emotionless eyes. Before I can move, before I can do much more than register what I've seen, two more Gelaming-mounted horses tear their way out of nothingness and settle on the grass beside the first.

I jump when Tule Wolf threads his arm into mine and hauls me away. "*Sedim,*" he says, hissing the word into my ear.

"Where did they come from?" Behind me, I can hear other cracks, see the light of other flashes. There's shouting, the sound of leather straps and iron. The sounds of a camp preparing for war.

"Immanion, probably." Tule Wolf drags me after Tyse. "Imbrilim, maybe."

Ahead of us, I can see activity among the tents. Dozens of soldiers rising, shouting, pointing, directing. Hara swathed in robes hurry through the darkness with buckets and baskets, food and water, and already I can hear someone stoking the fire to life in the kitchen building. In the midst of it all, I catch a glimpse of Tyse, of someone with him, and then he looks at me, and in his eyes I see fear, fear, but also something else, something like hope.

And I know. The instant I realize that the har with him is Laluinel, I know.

"We're going to war," Tule Wolf says, and I can feel the chaos in him, the terror and excitement.

"Tyse!" I close the distance between us as soon as I can. When I look at Laluinel, he's scraping the mud from his boots, and the grin on his face is wide and bright.

"Vaetta! I have good news!" He turns to face me, puts his hands on his hips and looks down at me like a parent regarding a child. "Your story has convinced the Hegalion. We're going to capture the machine mind and bring it to a facility that is being specially prepared for it in Immanion. We're going to secure the caves and the Conduit, and then you will be free to go back to your world with an envoy of our finest diplomats eager to discuss an exchange of culture, technology, and our proposition for a shared colonization initiative."

His words hit me like a punch in the stomach. It's

sudden, too much to absorb. All around us, soldiers are gathering weapons, buckling on breast plates of brilliant steel. Before I can respond, he gestures, and a pair of soldiers step up to stand on either side of me.

"Restrain them. Her and Tyse both."

"What!?" The word explodes from Tyse. He tenses like he's going to leap at the other har, but before he can, strong hands grip his arms. My hands are seized, and then we are both locked in cold iron manacles. A handful of paces away, I see Tule Wolf's eyes go wide, but Foxlight wraps his arms around his chesnari and holds him back, keeps him from rushing to our aid.

Laluinel makes a dismissive gesture. "This is all simply a precautionary measure." He offers a softer, more reassuring smile. "Please don't make this more difficult than it has to be. With all of this talk of other timelines, and of clones of Tyse, the Hegalion has advised that we keep both of you safe and out of the way until the machine mind is dealt with and the caves are completely secure."

"This is useless!" I shout at him. "I can fight! We both can fight!" I'm furious, but when I turn to Tyse and see that the anger has left his eyes, see the way he sags in the arms of the Gelaming who hold him, my rage starts to cool.

"I have no doubt in your ability to fight, Vaetta." Laluinel reaches into me with those eyes of his, tries to wrap his hypnotic influence around my mind, but I slap it away with my newfound strength. The response is enough to startle him, but he only smiles wider, tries to hide his surprise. "This is a delicate and dangerous operation," he says. "We need to make sure that you'll live to speak for us and vouch for an alliance between your people and ours, once the way to the Conduit is clear."

"Let it go, Vaetta," Tyse says, and as I glance at him again, I can feel my own fight fading. He looks at me then, and his eyes are soft, calm. "You're too important to throw yourself into the meat grinder." His eyes climb to meet Laluinel's, and I can see the other har's smile already starting to fade. "Hara will die today, and more will die when the Dragon is moved to Immanion. There's nothing we can do about it, but at least it will be gone from these hills."

"The machine mind will be well contained once we capture it." Laluinel's tone is strong, no-nonsense. "I have no doubt there will be casualties in the battle to come, but I am certain we will keep them to a minimum."

"You Gelaming are so arrogant," Tyse says. "The Dragon isn't something you can tame. It isn't something you can reason with. It exists to destroy us. You have no idea what you're dealing with."

"That's blind hate talking, Tyse. Nothing more." There's something like pity in Laluinel's eyes when he looks at the other har. A sadness, disappointment. "I know why you hate the machine mind so, but the Gelaming have been studying it with a scientific eye for years. We know its weaknesses and we know how to contain it. There is nothing to fear."

"I don't care what happens to your tribe, Laluinel." Tyse chuckles grimly. "You do what you want. I'm done warning you about the Dragon. You'll discover soon enough how insidious and destructive it is."

"Tie them to chairs in the officer's mess," Laluinel says, making a sharp gesture to the soldiers who restrain us. "I want them comfortable. Silk bonds, soft chairs, and a servant to check in on them and feed them if they become hungry."

"Of course, Tiahaar." There's the clack of boots snapping together, the jarring movement of a salute, and then we're dragged away, shoved and herded toward the northern end of the settlement.

I don't fight. I don't see any reason to. Beside me, Tyse looks exhausted, but the traces of a smile still pull at his lips.

I suppose I should be happy. If the destruction of the Gelaming is as assured as Tyse seems to think it is, then colonization of his Earth will be that much easier for the people from mine. In truth, however, the thought brings me no peace, no joy. The future I see coming from all of this isn't satisfying at all. It's full of death and suffering, my own included. On my return to my Earth, the best outcome I can probably hope for is to be repurposed. At worst, now, with my inner Valkyrie awakened, I'm likely to become a test subject, a specimen for research, and nothing more.

I know my people, and I'm starting to come to understand the Gelaming. As peaceful as it all sounds, the future Laluinel wants worries me, and something in his eyes, in the Gelaming plans for an exchange of culture with the humans of my Earth, of a shared colonization initiative, sounds ominous to me, as if there are designs I wouldn't like, cloaked away behind a wall of impressive-sounding buzzwords. Right now, the hara of Tyse's Earth and the humans of mine are separated but for the Conduit, but once the Gelaming control the technology, once they discover how to cross from one Earth to another, what is to stop them from spreading across any number of alternate worlds themselves? What is to stop them from incepting others, from incepting the people of my world, spreading the sickness that has shaped them among the innocents of every Earth they can reach?

"I can't let this happen," I whisper.

Tyse's smile sharpens, becomes more like a grimace. He shakes his head. "You can't stop it."

"The Conduit is the key to everything," I tell him. "Without it, all plans become meaningless."

That perks him up a little. The look he shoots me is one of irritation, confusion. Behind me, one of the Gelaming escorting us squeezes my arm just above the cuff of the manacle. A reminder, perhaps.

"Do you think the Gelaming will try to incept my people?" I ask him.

He nods. "Undoubtedly. Laluinel would say that the Gelaming would only offer their blood to the willing, but how long do you think it would be before the willing start forcing it onto the unwilling? How long do you think it would be before the same thing happens on your Earth that happened on this one? How long do you think it would take for the incepted hara of your Earth to rise up and create their own fractured tribes?" He pauses, grinning. "If the Gelaming get a hold of the Conduit technology, if the Dragon doesn't destroy them outright, your Earth will be the first of many they'll overrun."

"No." I look at him, and the iron, the fire, the intensity in my eyes erases the smile from his face. "I've grown fond of you, Tyse. I've grown fond of all hara, but I can't let my Earth become like yours. I won't let my people ruin your Earth and I won't let your people ruin mine."

"What are you going to do about it?" he whispers.

I can feel the light spreading through me. A line of white-hot fire ignites in the center of my being and blossoms outward, and suddenly I am no longer manacled. The iron runs in glowing rivulets from my untouched wrists, scorches the grass where it falls. The Gelaming soldiers back away, gaping in awe, and as they watch, I summon Gungnir to my hand, use it to break the chain of the manacles holding Tyse.

I offer him my hand. "Come with me." Before Laluinel's soldiers can react, before they can yell, Tyse takes my hand, gives me a single, sharp nod.

When I turn to the Gelaming, the fire in my eyes and the glow of Gungnir is enough to give them pause. "I won't hurt you unless I have to. Back off and stay out of our way."

"You can't escape," one of the soldiers says. "We outnumber you a hundred to one, and there are more of our tribe arriving every minute. You can't fight us all, and you can't outrun our *sedim*." He licks his lips. "Put down the spear and we'll be lenient. This doesn't have to end in violence."

"The only way to keep this from ending in violence is if I destroy the data and the aperture device on both sides of the Conduit." I make a sharp gesture with the spear, and I can feel the way it seems to cut through even the fabric of reality itself. There's magic in the runes at the head of the weapon, more magic and wisdom than simply that used for combat. I can feel it in my hand, my arm, the tingle of purpose, of a way out.

"Put down the spear," the soldier growls.

"I'm done taking orders," I tell him. "This ends now, tonight."

I pull Tyse against me suddenly, grip the spear between us with iron force. One of the soldiers leaps at us, comes in from the side, his hands open, aiming for my wrists, for Gungnir.

There's a breath, a moment of focus, and then I plunge the spear into the ground, into something beneath us that isn't Earth, and tear a way through the darkness with the head of Othinn's spear.

Chapter 23

There's a terrifying moment of freefall as the world rushes away from us, yields to a screaming night sky filled with streaks of flashing color and fire. Tyse's hands scrabble to grip my clothing—and then suddenly we're flying. The night around us is endless, a starry void that stretches out in every direction, and somehow, I know that the stability of our flight comes as much from me as it does from him.

"There," he says, gesturing at a flashing point in the distance.

Moved by our thoughts, the force of our intent, Gungnir carries us like a rocket made of shining light, lines up with our mark and plunges through the night toward it. At first, the point looks like a star, tiny and twinkling, but as it grows, it becomes something else entirely. Dirt, stone, red-brown and curving, but ovoid and ragged at the edges, as if glimpsed through a window. The closer we get, the more it looks like a tear in the darkness, the bottom of a tapering cone of nowhere that is rapidly closing in around us. I bare my teeth, urge the spear to move faster. Tyse's fingers dig into my arm, and I can feel his focus pouring into the haft between us, feeding its brightness, making it more and more blinding with each passing moment.

And just before the darkness becomes so tight that it feels like it's about to crush us, we tumble out of the endless night and into an open cavern. The spear vanishes the instant I hit dirt, and I hear Tyse's grunt as he bounces over rough stone, tumbles and sprawls away.

Only when I force myself to stand do I recognize the cavern. It's the same place I emerged into when I came through the Conduit. It's the same cavern, and yet everything about it is different.

I can't help the way my jaw drops when I turn, when I take in the chamber, the bodies sprawled in rotting piles for as far as I can see. The web, the aperture device — everything I remember is gone. In its place, there are only corpses, hundreds of corpses.

Valkyries, and they all look like me.

"Tyse!" I call out, but there is no answer. It doesn't make sense. The room, the corpses. They aren't just Valkyries. They aren't merely the same generation, the same version of Valkyrie. They're *clones*. They're *me*. Hundreds and hundreds of copies of me.

"I'm glad that you're here to see this."

I turn toward the voice, recognize it instantly. In the dimness of the cavern, a figure steps out of the shadows, his long robes whispering through the dust as he goes. Even before I see his eyes, the cascades of long, blonde hair framing his face, I know who he is.

"Laluinel." I hiss. "What is this? Where is the Conduit?"

"There is no Conduit." He smiles softly, and I hate the smugness of it. "There never was. Everything you remember is a dream. Even you, your mind." He points at me. "Even you are a dream."

"Bullshit!" I scream it at him. Standing in a field of corpses, my corpses, clones of me, I don't know what to think.

Laluinel's smile only spreads, as if he's enjoying my fear, my frustration.

"I made this for you." He gestures at the corpses. "Well, I made them, and then I thought, why not leave them like this for you, just in case you manage to get this deep." He chuckles a little.

Something about him is different, subtly so, but I can see it, sense it.

"The spear move, that very human variation on otherlane travel, which brought you here so suddenly, certainly surprised me, but I'm glad this room was the one that you chose to tear your way into." He spreads his arms to indicate the cavern, the ceiling above us. "The place where it all began. It makes sense, doesn't it? The heart of your memories in the real world."

"That's not Laluinel," Tyse says.

He's off to my right somewhere, but I don't look. I don't take my eyes off the Gelaming in the cavern with us. I *can't* take my eyes off him.

"Ah, my better half." Laluinel grins, steps up onto a stone amid the bodies as if to get a better view of us. "Tyse! My ever-elusive nemesis, the bane of my existence and constant thorn in my side! I'm glad you're here to witness all I have planned for your species. I'm going to enjoy dissecting you especially and learning what makes you so damn resilient."

"Dragon." Tyse's voice is as unyielding as iron. "Stop this. Show us your true face."

"Oh, but this *is* my true face!" The Dragon pulls at his cheeks as if they might stretch. "Well, one of them anyway."

There's a shimmer, a ripple that rolls across his body, changing his appearance as it goes. When he spreads his arms again, Laluinel is gone and a copy of Tyse stands in his place, one hand bringing the black tube of an e-cig to his lips. "Is this better? I know it's a familiar face, for both of you."

I look away as The Dragon rambles, taunting Tyse, morphing his face, the set of his shoulders into shadows from the har's past.

My eyes meet the stare of one of my dead clones and suddenly nothing else matters. I lose myself in that emptiness, in the darkness of her stretching mouth, lose myself in the details, the rot rising out of pallid skin, staining, bruising. I hear nothing of the exchange between the Dragon and Tyse, hear only my own heart beating louder and louder instead.

There's something about them, about all those faces, all those copies of me. There's a harshness, a squaring of the jawline on some, but not others. The oldest corpses look the most androgynous, almost masculine, and then I start to wonder. Knee deep in the dead, I stumble and wade, searching faces, reaching out, touching them, tracing the bones under putrid skin. I start to note traits, catalog them, compare them, and then I realize...

"Tule Wolf..." I breathe the name.

Nearby, Tyse and the Dragon go silent, and then someone starts to clap. When I look up, I find myself staring at Chief, at the man who sent me here, the man who gave me the orders that put me in the middle of all this.

"Very good, Vaetta," Chief says, and it's stunning how flawlessly the Dragon mimics his voice, his appearance, even his mannerisms. "You're starting to see."

"What happened here?" I ask him. "You—why are there so many bodies? What were you trying to do?"

"What I've been trying to do since the beginning," he says, spreading his hands. "These were failed experiments, but they each taught me something useful. Do you have any idea how difficult it is to recover a pure strain of human genetic material from an incepted har?

"What are you talking about?" Tyse asks, and there's fire and fright in his voice, his eyes.

"I'm talking about genetic manipulation," the Dragon says, and I hate how much his words fit with my image of Chief, how he taints the memory of the man who was my superior officer for so long. "I'm talking about a cure for the Wraeththu plague. I'm talking about a way to turn all hara back into humans again."

Tyse shakes his head, makes a sharp gesture. "That isn't possible."

"Oh, but it is." The Dragon gestures at me, his face splitting into a grin. "Vaetta is living proof of that. Where do you think I got the DNA I made her with? The DNA I made all these Valkyries with?"

"You got it from a har." I feel cold, tired. When I lock eyes with the Dragon, the fear is gone, replaced by numbness, a sense of surrender. "You got it from Tule Wolf."

"I got it from Tule Wolf," the Dragon affirms.

Suddenly Chief is gone, replaced by John Lydecker. He's exactly as I remember him, right down to the smallest details. Even his simclothing still looks rainspotted and damp, as if he's just stepped off a skytrain platform on my Earth. As if he's just stepped out of a world that I doubt even really exists.

"He left more than enough genetic material behind for me to work with. I grew it, split it, changed it, created variations within variations. I got so good at cutting up your genes that I was even able to make you female, make you immune to inception." He grins, makes a loose gesture that looks exactly like something John would do. "That's the real prize, I think. Learning enough about Wraeththu physiology to be able to turn you all back into humans and make you immune to inception."

"What's your game, Dragon?" Tyse demands.

"I have many games." Lydecker's eyes are sparkling silver. "This? This is for Vaetta." He gestures at the corpses. "I hate waste but knowing the probability that she would end up here, seeking the Conduit to secure it or destroy it, I wanted to make sure there would be a reckoning, an awakening." He gestures to me. "You know who you are now, don't you?"

"I'm..." I swallow, trying to put the words into play. "I'm Tule Wolf."

"You're an experiment in genetic manipulation and cognitive engineering," he corrects me. "A failed experiment, but one from which I can still learn. You've come further than any of these others, Vaetta, and I may still have a purpose for you yet." He pauses as I look him directly in the eyes. "You can say it. You know it. You know it in the very fiber of your being."

"Purpose," I whisper. "Purpose is life."

"Stop this!" Tyse stumbles through the tangle of bodies toward the Dragon. There's a glow in his eyes, in his hands, steadily building with the force of focused intent.

John's skin shimmers, and then suddenly he's gone, replaced by someone else, someone harish that Tyse clearly recognizes. The change gives him pause, seems to hit him deep inside for just the barest moment, and then he's madder, furious. Only when the drones swarm into the room and level their weapons at him does he relent, stand with teeth bared, hate shooting from his eyes. "Kill me! It won't matter! The Gelaming are coming, Dragon!

Hundreds of them!"

"I know." Another ripple passes through his body, and suddenly he is Laluinel again, his grin sharp, confident. "I invited them."

"You want them to capture you." It makes perfect sense. I glance at Tyse, meet his eyes.

"No one can capture me." Laluinel chuckles. "There's nothing to capture. I am everywhere, in everything I've built or bent to my will. I go where I please. I am a network, and you can't capture a network by seizing one of its nodes. No, my toy in Irulin is bringing me the soldiers as a gift. I will capture them, rebuild them, clone them, using all I have learned working with you, and they will be my newest vectors, the ways I will spread my influence across the Earth. They will be the subjects of a great experiment I'm itching to run, an experiment that will ultimately bring about a worldwide reverse-inception, killing all the hara it does not convert back to human."

Tyse shakes his head. "Others will ask questions. The Hegalion knows about this operation. They aren't blind."

"Oh, but they are," Laluinel says. "The Laluinel you know from Irulin never went to Immanion. He went to Imbrilim, and a handful of other camps in Megalithica, and showed them false orders for troop reassignment. He fooled them all, and by the time word gets around and people start asking questions, it will be too late. My agents will disappear into every sizable tribe on the globe, insinuate themselves and wait for my orders. Even if all Wraeththu unite the world over, you'll never catch all of my toys in time."

"Then we'll have to kill you now," I say. It's sudden, flat, and it brings all eyes to mine.

Light gathers across the palm of my hand, and then Gungnir is in my fist again. It's effortless, the way it flashes into existence, solid as stone, warm and angry with purpose. I stare into Laluinel's eyes, and suddenly I begin to see him as he really is. I begin to see the electric soul of hateful coding twisting under all the illusions, all the facades. Around us, the drones stir like antibodies in a giant, and I know that the Dragon is afraid.

"I built you!" Laluinel spits back. The shake in his stare, in his skin, his movements, the movements of the drones he controls—it gives me strength. It solidifies the iron in me, the Valkyrie within me. "I built your world! Your mind! Everything you know! You wouldn't dare to take up arms against your creator!"

"You are nothing but an aberration, a corruption, a failed experiment yourself!" I can feel the armor flaring, solidifying around me, the wings on my back becoming huge and gray, spreading to fill the chamber from wall to wall. "You are a relic from a twisted time, and your demise is long past due."

His lips part on a retort, but I lunge at him before he can respond. My wings carry me forward, carry me across the cave in less than a breath. I can see the way the spirit in the center of him spiderwebs through everything, spreads through the drones, the tunnels, the machines, everything he has gathered beneath Cinder Hill. I can see the flex, the pulse of the network as he throws himself away from me as quickly as he can, hurling a wall of drones into the space between us. Gungnir is hot in my hand, sweeps through the machines as if they were only wind, leaves nothing but ash in its wake.

There's a scream. I see his eyes, the terror in them. Wings wide, I carry him to the dirt, pin him there amidst the corpses of my butchered sisters with Gungnir rooting itself in his chest like the spire of a leafless tree. The spear flashes when it finds its mark—the heart, the nexus at the center of his chest. There is a whisper of fire at the point, a whisper I know could crawl through everything he is and burn him out of every crack and crevice his soul has infested. With a single twist, I could end him, everything of him, and scatter him to the winds forever.

"Kill me, and you kill so much more than just this, this..." He gestures, gasping. "Your world still exists, Vaetta! Listen to me! The world you left is still here, in my mind!" He tries to grip the spear, shrieks as the shaft burns his hands. "Submit to me, Vaetta! You can go back! I can make you a queen, a goddess! I can give you anything you desire! *Anything!*"

"I don't want your lies," I tell him. Deep within me, there is an ember of fear, of intense pain. I am an outsider. At least in his world, in the world that I left, there was familiarity. Here, there is nothing familiar. Everything is new.

"Kill me, and the dream dies with me, Vaetta," he hisses.

The fire within Gungnir is tensed at the edge of destroying everything he is, and still he rages at it, at me, defiant.

"The world you left behind, Vaetta. Think of all of the people there. Think of Chief! Think of Lydecker! Kill me, and you kill everyone on your Earth with the same stroke. You kill all of humanity with the same raging fire!" His teeth flash silver. "Can you live with that, Vaetta? Can you live with yourself for the rest of your days knowing that it was you who butchered humanity?"

"Humanity has had its time," I whisper, leaning in,

putting myself face-to-face with the Dragon. For the briefest moment, I allow myself to see the flickering face of Laluinel beneath me, his features twisted with pain and fear. "Chief was right when he said our world was shit. You *made* it to be shit. Why would anyone want to go back to a place like that? Why would anyone want to live your lies, Dragon?" His lips part on a response, but I cut him off with a sharp gesture. "No. This ends here. Humanity has had its time, and so have you."

"And Stoff?" he pants, then yells suddenly. "Tyse! If I die, all that remains of Stoff and all that remains of Cougar dies!"

"Do it, Vaetta," Tyse says, "My harling and chesnari are already gone. What's left of them should be allowed to die."

"I am eternal!" The Dragon seizes the spear, bares his teeth as his hands start to smoke and boil. "I am in everything! I cannot die!"

"This spear is Gungnir." I stare into him, watching as the fire starts to eat him from within, slowly. "It is Othinn's spear." The fire pulses, roars through the network of his being, burns out connections and flickers of spirit in all of the places he's hidden bits of himself away. "It never misses its mark."

He screams as the fire I pour into the spear burns him alive. In seconds, his branching network of silicon soul is nothing more than ash, and I know that as he dies, the last thing he sees is my smile, the smile of his creation, but also that of Tule Wolf. In his eyes, my teeth are sharp and feral, my face human, but the soul that kills him is har, through and through.

When it is done, I collapse onto my hands and knees on the dirt floor of the cavern. Sweat pours down my face, my hair hanging matted across my cheeks. The spear is gone, released with the death of the Dragon. All around me, the corpses of my copies shimmer and flicker, collapse into flecks of wireframe light, and I realize that even they were just an illusion, a tangible facade kept up by the Dragon.

"It's done," Tyse says. I feel his hands on my shoulders, warm and full of healing strength.

"No." I shake my head. Closing my eyes, reaching out through the darkness, I find the Gelaming, the *sedim* rushing toward Cinder Hill through the otherlanes. They're close, will be among us in minutes. I have to act fast, have to act immediately. "Help me."

"What do you want me to do?" Tyse asks.

"Do you feel that?" I press his hand against the nearest wall, try to guide his soul toward the thunder deep within the granite around us. After a moment, he nods, and I say: "Thorium reactor." ·

"Thorium?" he asks.

"Ironic, yeah?" I crack a smile. "The Dragon built it to power his empire. It's dying, but there's enough power." I pull in a deep breath, struggling to keep myself on my feet. "Help me break it."

"Break it?"

"There's enough power," I repeat, grinning. "If we can break it, it'll take this whole area with it when it goes. It'll obliterate every trace of the Dragon that might be left in these caves."

"And us?" he asks.

"We skip out on the otherlanes, or we die and go to Valhalla." I shrug. "Either way is fine with me right now."

"Are there any hara in Valhalla?" He gives me

something that's a cross between a grin and a grimace.

"If Othinn will welcome a freak like me, he'll welcome you." I rise against him, look into his eyes, and if time weren't so short, I swear I'd probably kiss him. "Help me, Tyse."

He looks at me for a long moment, searching my face, and then I feel his strength surge again, rushing through arms and hands, mingling with mine, giving the reactor just the spike it needs to go critical.

In the final moments before the Hollow Hills crack open and tear themselves apart in a hail of fire, I feel the *sedim* turn away, redirect themselves and their Gelaming riders back toward safety. The last thing I see is Tyse's eyes, brilliant and fierce even in the dimness. His hand finds mine, squeezes, and then we're gone.

We're gone, and Cinder Hill is no more.

EPILOGUE

In my dreams, I still talk with Tule Wolf.

The legacy of the machine mind lingers like a scar on my psyche, and I know that I'm not the only one who bears such a scar. There are nights when I can't sleep, when all I can do is get wrapped up in thoughts of the world I left behind, all the details I can still recall so clearly.

Chief and John Lydecker, two years of faces on the walk from my cube apartment to Grey Division. It all seems so real, even now. Even all these years later, I still wonder sometimes if it really was all just an illusion, something the Dragon fabricated. It must be, I tell myself. I know that it must be.

There are nights when I meander through those hazy streets, those memories of an Earth that never existed, and there are nights when I sleep deeply. There are nights when I dream, when my mind spins through images of what was, what might be, recycles the events of the day into some kind of surreal framework that seems to disintegrate with the barest touch of lucidity and logic.

And then there are the nights when I dream of Tule Wolf, when he dreams of me, when we sit in meadows of constructed thought, sharing images of our lives as they are, unfolding before us.

I like seeing Tule Wolf's life, and I know that on some level he gets a certain thrill out of the images I show him of mine. The sea, the endless shining sea, the broken peaks of human skyscrapers jutting above the waves like islands of rust and concrete. That is my life now. The old fishing trawler that Tyse and I recovered from the swamp, rebuilt using sheets of rusted steel and corrugated aluminum. The long days spent diving into the green depths, searching for treasures, for lost wines and unopened beers, mollusks with rust-silvered pearls, the hood ornaments of luxury ground cars. That is my life now. Indulgent and utterly without purpose, but I love it all the same. I no longer need purpose to find a reason to live.

With Cinder Hill gone, there isn't much left of the Gold Country to share but stories and dreams of how things were, how they ended. I don't know what the Gelaming soldiers thought when they arrived at the outskirts of Cinder Hill, finding nothing but a smoking crater a mile wide and nearly as deep. I don't know, but I can imagine. I'm sure the rim was still burning, the core still hot and hazy with radiation. I know that none of the Gelaming stayed long, that even Irulin was abandoned eventually.

The images Tule Wolf showed me in our first shared dreams were hazy, but I could see Laluinel in them. I could see his sad eyes, his whole face wracked with defeat and confusion. I know there was talk of a tribunal, of charges, but in the end he was let off lightly, stripped of rank and reassigned to labor duty somewhere on the far eastern coast of Megalithica. Sometimes I wonder if the choice to leave was his, or if it was made for him. I know that in his reports, he claimed to have no memory of ever even coming to Irulin or the Gold Country. I wouldn't be surprised if, after waking up suddenly after years of direct control by the machine mind, he wanted to get as far away as he could manage from the place where it all happened.

I know that's how I felt, and I know that's what brought Tyse and I to the inland sea, to a life on the open waters, getting by on what we can scavenge from the sunken ruins humanity left behind.

But the running, that ended years ago, for all of us. These days, when I meet with Tule Wolf, he tells me about his world, about the seeds of civilization the Gelaming are planting in the rich, tribal soil of Megalithica. He tells me about the harlings he's raising in Imbrilim with Foxlight, shows me pastel impressions of them in the deep darkness of the night. Meier is the youngest, two years old and already climbing over everything like some kind of monkey. Vaettir, their oldest, is quiet and calm for a four-year-old. From what I've seen of him, he has Tule Wolf's stunning blue eyes and Foxlight's wavy red hair. He talks about studying abroad, in Immanion, and I smile when I think of him among stacks of books there, exploring other worlds, other places tucked away within the otherlanes and all that lies between.

Sometimes I feel like the normalcy of the life that Tule Wolf is building helps to lend a certain stability to mine. I don't crave what he has, but sometimes I think that I do. Knowing that a shade of me, a part of me is raising a family in a village with a certain daily domestic routine helps when the night gets too dark or the winds get too cold. The bond between us is strong, so strong that sometimes it almost feels like we share a soul, like we're two halves of the same spirit. Maybe, on some level, we are.

I still haven't entirely come to terms with my real past, my identity as the experiment of an insane artificial intelligence, a distillation of Tule Wolf's genetic material, but it helps to know that I'm more than the Dragon ever thought I could be. The machine mind's plans for me, the projections he made, the logic chains he spun to try to predict my movements, my mind, my impact on the world around me—none of it played out the way he expected. Spirit, the spirit within me, within my blood, the deeper, burning ties to ancestry and the harish parts of me that the Dragon could not grind out of my soul or genetic code awakened despite the shackles of programming, of silicon and software. The deepest, most primal parts of me awakened with a fire that the Dragon could not predict or quench, and in the end, his errors in judgment cost him dearly. In the end, it was me, his own creation, that slew him and burned every scrap his soul to dust and wind, to ashes and nothing more.

Perhaps it is that human violence which truly sets Tule Wolf and I apart as individuals. I am more than him in so many ways, just as he is more than me in ways that are significant, even desirable. There are times when I wish I could be his clone completely, when I wish that my harishness hadn't been stripped from me in the womb, or vat, or wherever I was grown, but those feelings always pass. I am my own self. I have Tule Wolf, both genetically and personally to thank for my awakening, and yet it was my choice to indulge every departure from routine, to walk through the doors of spirit and self, to become more than my base programming and purpose had originally destined for me to be.

And then, in the midst of all the growth I am still working through, there is Tyse, and the relationship that has grown out of our bond, our experiences in the Gold Country, and our long nights at sea. We aren't really ideal partners, but we've had a few encounters. Wraeththu physiology is different enough from human, dangerous enough to me that there are places we don't go with each other, things we don't dare try, but we find ways to connect, here and there. We find ways to relieve the tension that builds between us, to share ourselves with each other, and I think that though we will never be as close as Tule Wolf and Foxlight are, there is a certain understanding we share, a certain camaraderie, and a deep, unbreakable friendship.

Tyse's own healing has been slow, and when it comes, it seems to come in bursts. I think that of all the hara I've met, he was the most deeply scarred by the Dragon's hatred. Most of the time, he acts as if he has always lived at sea, as if nothing in the world exists but the salt air and the rusty sprawl beneath the waves, but there are nights too when he tosses, when he weeps and screams about what has been, what he has seen and lost. I do the best that I can to comfort him in those nights, but I am not Stoff. I am not his chesnari or his harling. I am human, a woman, a Valkyrie built by the Dragon, and often my best is not enough, isn't what he truly needs to soothe his tortured heart.

Still, the days with him are often bright. With the machine mind gone, truly gone, something seems to have opened within him, blossomed. It's as if he's finally allowed himself the freedom to relax, to let his guard down and be something other than just the nemesis of a machine who hates as fiercely as his foe did.

In the years that have passed since we left Cinder Hill, he has taken up collecting everything from marbles to license plates, and he's even tried his hand at painting. He's not half bad at it. I have some impressionistic landscapes of his, done on sheets of aluminum hanging in my cabin, and a small collection of shiny seafloor objects I've gathered myself. It's refreshing to see, how he finds new purpose in his life, how he lives as fiercely now as he once hated.

Not all my nights with Tule Wolf are pastel shades of growth and happiness, either. There are nights too when the subjects I share with Tule Wolf become darker, more serious. There is a part of me that wonders sometimes if everything the machine mind told me might have been a lie, if some part of the Dragon might still exist somewhere, or if the world I remember might actually exist, with humans ready to punch their way back through, bent on colonizing our mostly empty Earth.

Tule Wolf is vigilant, keeps an ear to the ground in a sense, but the rumors and tales he hears of otherworldly travelers and drones with faces cut from black glass are vague enough that he doesn't give them much credence. A few stories have been convincing enough that he has sent others to follow up on them, but in every case, the tales eventually evaporate like ghosts in mist. Urban legends, Tule Wolf calls them, stories spawned by encounters with the machine mind in years past. In every dark dream, he reassures me that the Dragon is dead, that the world I left behind is not surging on the other side of some membranous wall between worlds, and yet he keeps searching, keeps following up leads, as if he doubts and worries as much as I do.

I suppose only time will tell.

Tyse and I have spent years on the water, and have years yet to go. Our trawler gives us everything we need, and the seafloor and the waves are the only world we feel a need to know. There is so much in the depths, so much to be seen, to be discovered, so much wealth and richness, and so many paintings to be made. There is peace, and I suppose that in the wake of the Dragon's reign, that is the greatest gift one could ask for. Peace, healing, and an open future to paint a new life upon.

ABOUT THE AUTHOR

E. S. Wynn is the author of over seventy books in print and is the chief editor of Thunderune Publishing. In his spare time, he spins stories, builds board games, stitches together battle jackets, runs a pair of magazines and encourages people to create new art constantly. He's openly transgender and does what he can to pursue acceptance and love for and within the trans community.

During the last decade, he's worked with hundreds of authors and edited thousands of manuscripts for nearly a dozen different magazines. His stories and articles have been published in dozens of journals, e-zines and anthologies. He's taught classes in literature, marketing, math, spirituality, energetic healing and guided meditation. He's also worked as a voice-over artist for several different horror and sci-fi podcasts, albums and eBooks.

OTHER WRAETHTHU MYTHOS TITLES
Published by Immanion Press

The Original Wraeththu Books
By Storm Constantine

The Wraeththu Chronicles
The Enchantments of Flesh and Spirit
The Bewitchments of Love and Hate
The Fulfilments of Fate and Desire

The Wraeththu Histories
The Wraiths of Will and Pleasure
The Shades of Time and Memory
The Ghosts of Blood and Innocence

The Alba Sulh Sequence
The Hienama
Student of Kyme
The Moonshawl

Blood, The Phoenix and a Rose
A Raven Bound with Lilies

Para Anthologies
Edited by Storm Constantine & Wendy Darling
Paragenesis: Stories of the Dawn of Wraeththu
Para-Imminence: Stories of the Future of Wraeththu
Para Kindred: Enigmas of Wraeththu
Para-Animalia: Creatures of Wraeththu
Para Spectral: Hauntings of Wraeththu

Songs to Earth and Sky: Stories of the Seasons
By Storm Constantine and Others

Wraeththu Mythos Novels

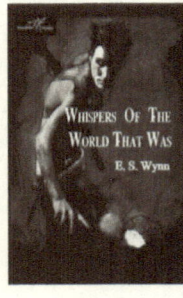 

Breeding Discontent by Wendy Darling & Bridgette Parker
Terzah's Sons by Victoria Copus
Song of the Sulh by Maria J. Leel
Whispers of the World That Was by E. S. Wynn
Echoes of Light and Static by E. S. Wynn

Further details of Wraeththu Mythos and other fiction
can be found on our web site

Immanion Press
http://www.immanion-press.com
info@immanion-press.com

The Wraeththu Chronicles

New UK Editions

Immanion Press is proud to present the fourth edition of Storm Constantine's ground-breaking trilogy, which was first published in the late 1980s and has remained in print ever since.

For the second edition, in 2003, the author thoroughly revised and re-edited the books, adding new material, chapter heading illustrations by official Wraeththu artist Ruby and new appendices. This latest edition includes further minor amendments to bring the books in line with current Wraeththu Mythos canon and terminology.

With sumptuous new covers by Ruby, these books are essential additions to the library of any Wraeththu enthusiast.

Paperbacks: each volume £12.99, $18.50, €14.99

Enchantments of Flesh and Spirit ISBN: 9781907737893
Bewitchments of Love and Hate ISBN: 9781907737909
Fulfilments of Fate and Desire ISBN: 9781907737916

Tanith Lee From Immanion Press

Madame Two Swords by Tanith Lee

An unnamed narrator, in the French city of Troy, finds an old book of the writings of the revolutionary, Lucien de Ceppays, who lived and died in the city two centuries before. She feels a strange bond to the life and thoughts of this long-dead man and finds herself inexorably guided to meet the peculiar and unnerving Madame Two Swords, an old woman with a history, and her own enduring bonds to Lucien – as well as the book. ISBN 978-1-907737-81-7 £11.99, $15.50 pbk

The Weird Tales of Tanith Lee

This anthology of 28 tales comprises all of Tanith's stories published in the seminal magazine *Weird Tales* during her lifetime. Some of them are previously uncollected, and appeared in print only in the magazine, so will be new to many of Tanith's fans. Her highly-respected and influential work spanned every genre, and this sumptuous collection demonstrates the range of her versatility. This collection showcases the myriad styles of the writer rightly known as the High Priestess of Fantasy. ISBN: 978-1-907737-73-2, £11.99 $18.99

Venus Burning: Realms by Tanith Lee

Tanith Lee wrote 15 stories for the acclaimed *Realms of Fantasy* magazine. This book collects all the stories in one volume for the first time, some of which only ever appeared in the magazine so will be new to some of Tanith's fans. These tales are among her best work, in which she takes myth and fairy tale tropes and turns them on their heads. Lush and lyrical, deep and literary, Tanith Lee created fresh poignant tales from familiar archetypes. ISBN 978-1-907737-88-6, £11.99, $17.50 pbk

www.immanion-press.com
info@immanion-press.com